The Student's Cookbook

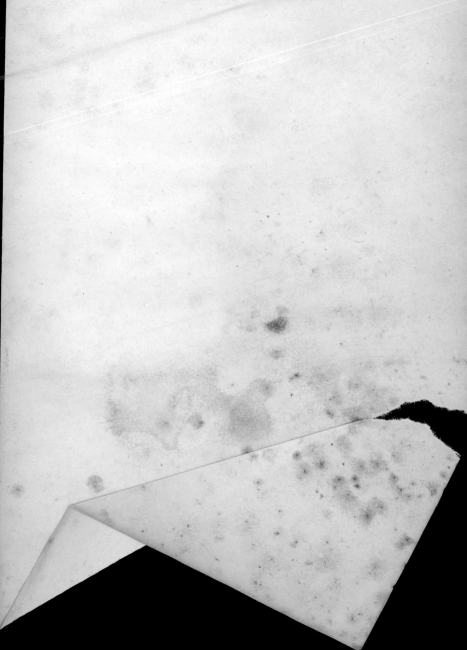

THE STUDENT'S COOKBOOK

Jenny Baker

faber and faber

LONDON · BOSTON

First published in 1985
by Faber and Faber Limited
3 Queen Square London WC1N 3AU
Reprinted in 1987, 1988, 1989 and 1990

Printed in Great Britain by
Cox & Wyman Ltd, Reading, Berkshire
All rights reserved

British Library Cataloguing in Publication Data

Baker, Jenny
The student's cookbook
1. Low budget cookery
I. Title
641.5'52   TX652
ISBN 0–571–13522–6

Library of Congress Cataloging in Publication Data

Baker, Jenny
The student's cookbook
1. Cookery   I. Title.
TX652.B3124   1985   641.5   85–1544
ISBN 0–571–13522–6 (pbk.)

For Mark and Madeleine

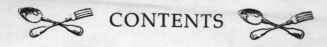

CONTENTS

INTRODUCTION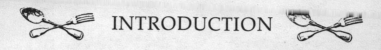

This book was first begun because of the needs of four particular students: Mark, Madeleine, Trisha and Tony. All of them were living on their own for the first time and were faced with the task of feeding and looking after themselves. I began by simply jotting down recipes which I thought they might find useful. I soon realized this was not enough. They needed not just recipes but ideas for making meals out of quite simple ingredients that wouldn't involve them in too much time or money. And so although there are recipes in this book, I have also devoted a lot of space to variations on different themes. My hope is that you will use these to trigger off your own ideas.

You're going to have to feed yourself on a tight budget. That grant cheque which first time round seems like quite a windfall, very soon dwindles once you've covered other essentials such as rent, heating and lighting, books and equipment, fares, pocket money and clothes. The good news for students is that it is possible to live very well on some of the less costly ingredients. In fact many of the foods that are now considered bad for you come in the more expensive range. So take heart, you don't after all have to starve even though you might be living in a garret. Sometimes you will want to throw off all thoughts of poverty and splash out on something really extravagant and so I have included some luxuries. It isn't much fun to buy, say, a steak and then have it end up on your plate tasting like an old piece of leather because you don't know how to cook it.

Cooking is a creative process and there are as many ways of doing things as there are cooks. This isn't a textbook on cookery but I've had to assume that some people won't have done very much cooking in their lives; so bear with me if sometimes I tell you things which seem obvious.

I hope this book will give you lots of ideas and, if you have never cooked before, will open up a whole new aspect of life.

So, good cooking and good eating!

Part 1

BASICS

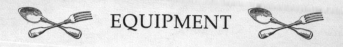

EQUIPMENT

You may be lucky and find yourself living somewhere with a fully equipped kitchen; the chances are you will have to buy some items yourself. Different people have different ideas, so the list below should be taken as a guide to the sort of things I think you would find useful. There's no need to rush out and buy everything on it, it's more practical and much more fun to add to your arsenal as and when you need to. There's a huge range of kitchen equipment to be found in chain stores, specialist shops, department stores and supermarkets; and sometimes you can find a real bargain in a charity shop or at a jumble sale.

IMPLEMENTS

Corkscrew and bottle opener

Egg whisk   *You can manage with a fork, but a balloon-shaped wire whisk speeds up the process and increases the amount of air incorporated.*

Knife   *A really sharp knife is a must. Choose a cook's knife, the best you can afford.*

Non-stick spatula or fish slice   *Made of plastic or special surface, will not scratch non-stick pans as will metal implements.*

Plastic slotted spoon   *Useful for stir-frying.*

Potato masher

Rubber spatula   *Used for scraping the last morsel out of a pan or bowl.*

Scissors

Tin opener

Vegetable peeler   *Handy for peeling vegetables really thinly and more effective than using a knife. Can also be used for slicing cheese. Look out for the swivel-bladed variety; once you've mastered the technique of peeling away from yourself with quick, light strokes, you'll find it a great aid.*

Wooden spoon and fork   *Useful for stirring soups, sauces, pasta, rice, etc.*

GRATERS AND STRAINERS

Cheese grater   *Either metal and box-shaped or flat, or a Mouli-grater for cheese, breadcrumbs, etc.*
Colander   *For straining vegetables, pasta, the contents of cans, etc.*
Mouli-légumes   *A useful gadget which is supplied with three different blades for grating, mashing and shredding. It works by hand, fits over a bowl or pan and is good for puréeing soups.*
Pepper mill   *Used for grinding black peppercorns; pepper dispensed in this way is vastly superior to the ready-ground variety.*
Sieve   *Can be used as a strainer. If you're baking, sieving the flour helps to aerate it and makes for a lighter dish.*
Spatter screen   *Used to cover a frying pan to prevent grease spattering everywhere. Can also be used for straining and steaming.*

MEASURING EQUIPMENT

Set of plastic measuring spoons   *The spoon measurements in this book are based on standard sizes which are marked on spoon sets in millilitres; a teaspoon is 5 ml, a dessertspoon is 10 ml and a tablespoon is 15 ml.*
Mug   *One which holds 16 tablespoons of liquid, or half a pint.*
Cook's measuring jug   *One that gives solid and liquid measures. See-through kinds make it easier to measure accurately. Especially handy when using recipes which are given in weights or fluid amounts.*

POTS AND PANS, BAKING TINS, ETC.

Frying pan   *An 18-cm (7-inch) pan with a non-stick coating would be ideal for one person. You might need one of about 25 cm (10 inches) when cooking for more; you could consider a wok (see page 18) as an alternative to this larger size, although you won't be able to use this for all frying purposes. If you have a frying pan with a non-stick base you can use minimum oil or fat and the pan is easy to clean. Make sure you don't use metal tools with this type of pan as they will damage the surface, and don't use scouring pads or powders.*

Saucepans *Two or three, ranging in size from 1–3 litres (2–6 pints). Non-stick or enamel coated are easy to clean. Heavy-based pans are best as they are less likely to burn.*

Casserole *You'll need this if you are pot roasting or making lots of stews. A heavy-based enamelled cast-iron pan is ideal and could double up as your third large saucepan and be used for cooking rice, spaghetti, etc. If you want one for oven cooking only, an earthenware pot would be suitable; some can also be used on top of the stove, these have unglazed bases, but you should check when you buy.*

Baking sheet *If you are cooking pastry, it will help to speed up the cooking time and crisp the underside. Useful for pizzas, foil parcels, baking potatoes, etc.*

Grill pan with grid *Most stoves come complete with this but if there isn't one, you'll find it useful to buy one.*

Loaf tin *The 1-litre (2-pint) size is useful for breads, gratins, meat loaves, Yorkshire puddings.*

Potato baker *A gadget on which you impale potatoes to reduce cooking time by about 15 minutes. You could use skewers or a stainless steel fork instead.*

Roasting tin *Necessary if you want to cook roast meats.*

Shallow oven dish *In tin, ovenproof glass or pottery, for gratins, pancake dishes, lasagne, etc.*

Tin or ring for savoury flans *An 18-cm (7-inch) removable-base tin, or a ring which is used on a baking sheet for quiches and pizzas.*

MISCELLANEOUS

Bowls *One or two for mixing. Half-litre and litre (1- and 2-pint) sizes would be useful. Pudding basins are a good shape for beating eggs, etc.*

Cling film, foil, greaseproof paper, kitchen paper roll *All are extremely handy to have in the kitchen.*

Jug or pot for coffee *Useful if making real coffee.*

Rolling pin *The most efficient is a long, handleless kind. If desperate, use a bottle.*

Tea pot *Saves on the tea bags if you're always serving tea to friends.*

Timer   *Very useful if you are inclined to be thinking of other things.*
Wide-mouthed insulated flask   *The ¼- or ½-litre (½- or 1-pint) size for making yogurt or keeping soup hot for a packed lunch.*
Wooden or melamine cutting board   *You need a flat surface on which to cut, and it can double as a board for rolling pastry. You might find an off-cut at a DIY shop. Useful size would be about 45 × 30 cm (18 × 12 inches).*

PRESENT LIST

There are other more expensive items which you might find useful, none of which are essential for the recipes in this book. However, they are worth considering as items for a Christmas list. They all come with their own instructions, so I have limited myself to listing them with a few simple comments.
Blender   *As well as being useful for puréeing soups, it can be used for making sauces, including mayonnaise, mixing up egg mixtures for quiche fillings, making breadcrumbs, chopping nuts, carrots, parsley, etc., grinding coffee beans, mixing party drinks, mixing up milk made from water and skimmed milk powder.*
Chinese wok   *Extremely useful for stir-frying vegetables and making quick dishes. Food is cut up and cooked over high heat in very little oil. It's a good idea to get one of at least 38 cm (15 inches) diameter, because even when cooking only small quantities of food, the curved shape of the base ensures the food uses minimum oil and maximum heat; if cooking large amounts you need the space to toss the food. If you're able to find a Chinese shop selling woks, they will be a great deal cheaper than those found in specialist kitchen shops. You'll need the pan, a lid and, if you are cooking on an electric hob, a base on which the pans rests while on the stove.*
Food processor   *Does a multitude of cooking chores: chopping, grinding, blending, mixing, mincing, slicing and shredding, making doughs and pastry, puréeing soups and sauces. This could well be at the top of your Christmas list if you find you are really doing a lot of cooking.*
Kettle   *An electric kettle saves on time but is expensive to run. However, if you have limited cooking facilities, it would be useful, especially the jug-type shape, as you do save on fuel by only boiling exactly the amount you need. The old type has an element which must*

always be covered with water and you therefore often have to boil more than you will use.

Multicooker   *If your cooking facilities are very limited, this electric cooking pan would be a godsend. It will fry, grill, roast and bake.*

Pressure cooker   *Cooking time is greatly reduced, so this is useful if you make lots of stews or casseroles and cook your own pulses.*

Sandwich maker   *A handy gadget if other facilities are limited.*

Slow-cooker   *Cooks at a very low temperature and is therefore cheap on electricity. Can be used for soups, stews, vegetables, cakes and puddings. The cooking process can take up to 10 hours, so you must be prepared to plan ahead. Especially useful if cooking for lots of people.*

QUANTITIES,
MEASUREMENTS AND
TEMPERATURES

QUANTITIES

The recipes in this book are for 1 person unless otherwise stated. If increasing quantities for more than one, be careful about additional seasoning. You won't need twice as much salt, for example, when preparing for two. So taste as you go.

Appetites vary, so you may find you need to prepare a little more or less than I have suggested.

MEASUREMENTS

More and more packaged food is being marked with metric weights and measures as well as those based on the imperial system. Eventually the imperial system is destined to become obsolete but until that happens we are in a state of some confusion. In an effort to try and make life simpler for you, I have worked out the quantities in the recipes using either spoons or mugs wherever possible. Occasionally I have deviated from this rule when it is obviously simpler to gauge a quantity in a different way. For example as milk comes in pint containers, I refer to a pint of milk. And food that you will buy loose, such as meat and vegetables, is given in both metric and imperial quantities.

The spoons I have used are based on a standard set of measuring spoons. These usually come complete with ½ teaspoon, teaspoon, dessertspoon and tablespoon sizes and are marked in millilitres; the teaspoon being 5 ml, the dessertspoon 10 ml, and the tablespoon 15 ml.

The mug I have used is a half-pint beer mug. Most mass-produced mugs are also equivalent to half a pint.

A pinch is literally that, the amount you can pinch between your finger and thumb, it's equivalent to about ⅛ teaspoon.

In order to measure an exact level spoon or mug, fill it generously and then take the blade of a knife across the top to remove the surplus. All measures are level unless otherwise stated.

You may prefer to use a weights system rather than one based on spoons and mugs. Below you will find a table which converts some spoon and mug measures into ounces and grams. You might find it useful when using recipes contained in other books. A word of warning. Imperial measures don't convert very comfortably into metric ones, for instance 1 ounce is equivalent to 28.3 grams – so an approximate nearest figure has to be taken and adjustments must be made as you multiply upwards. So when following recipes use either metric or imperial, don't mix the two. Recipes are always worked out proportionately.

SPOON AND MUG CONVERSIONS

Honey Jam Syrup Treacle	1 tablespoon = 1 oz or 25 grams approx.	a ½-pint mug = 10 oz or 275 grams approx.
Fats Oil Rice Sugar	2 tablespoons = 1 oz or 25 grams approx.	a ½-pint mug = 8 oz or 225 grams approx.
Cocoa Cornflour Flour	3 tablespoons= 1 oz or 25 grams approx.	a ½-pint mug = 6 oz or 175 grams approx.
Breadcrumbs Grated cheese Oats	4 tablespoons = 1 oz or 25 grams approx.	a ½-pint mug = 4 oz or 100 grams approx.

Liquid measures:
   1 pint is equivalent to 20 fluid ounces
   1 litre is equivalent to 35 fluid ounces
   1¾ pints is equivalent to a litre

Weights:

    1 pound is equivalent to 450 grams approx.

    1 kilogram is equivalent to 2.2 pounds

OVEN TEMPERATURES

Oven temperatures are given for gas regulo marks, electric Fahrenheit and Celsius. Below is a conversion table which you might find useful.

		Gas	°Fahrenheit	°Celsius
Very low	{	$\frac{1}{4}$	225	110
		$\frac{1}{2}$	250	120
Low	{	1	275	140
		2	300	150
Moderate	{	3	325	160
		4	350	180
Moderately hot	{	5	375	190
		6	400	200
Hot	{	7	425	220
		8	450	230
Very hot		9	475	240

If you are using an electric oven, it is necessary to preheat it for 10 or 15 minutes before putting in your dish. Food can be put straight into a gas oven from cold, but you should increase the cooking time by about 10 minutes. Ovens do vary so you may find you have to modify slightly the times given in the recipes. You'll very soon get the feel of your oven. Cultivate your nose! Your sense of smell is a very good guide as to when something is done or about to burn.

SOME NOTES ON USING A COOKER

This is perhaps the point to tell you that it is cheaper to use the top of the stove than the grill, and it is cheaper to use the grill rather than the oven. So if you are keen to economize, plan to use the oven when you have several things you want to cook, or perhaps on days when several of you are going to cook. Sometimes you'll really fancy jacket potatoes or maybe you won't have time to keep an eye on things, so you'll use the oven anyway. It will still be cheaper to do this than to go out and buy a take-away. You can save money too on fuel by always covering pans you are bringing to the boil and if you're using a kettle by only using sufficient water for your needs.

GOOD FOOD

What is good food and what is a good diet? More and more people are becoming concerned about the effects that certain foods have on ourselves and also on the world around us. As a student you are in a unique position. You are at a time in your life when you are most open to change and as you are most probably living away from home, you are no longer dependent on other people to plan your meals and dictate the type of food you must eat. With current research suggesting that certain of our most familiar foods are not all that good for us, it might be helpful for you to have an idea of the sort of diet to aim for.

Avoid if you can too many foods that are high in animal fats, sugar and salt. Fat is a necessary part of our diet but we can cut down on animal-fat intake by using instead those fats and oils which are labelled as polyunsaturated. It is also worth limiting the amount of ready-prepared foods that we eat because they too may be high in animal fats. Sugar has been known as the provider of energy but we now know that a better supply of energy can be obtained from eating foods high in carbohydrates, such as bread — especially wholemeal — potatoes and cereals.

Until recently these foods were labelled as being the chief reasons for weight gain. In fact, sugar and foods with a high fat content are the ones to be avoided if you are trying to lose weight. Salt is used in many packaged and ready-made goods, so to limit our intake it is sensible to cut down on the amount we add to our own dishes, as well as to taste things before adding more when either cooking or on your plate.

The table on page 25 shows how to identify some good sources of protein, carbohydrate and fat. On page 26 I have listed some of the foods which are best eaten less frequently, because they contain high amounts of animal fats, sugar or salt. Provided you vary your diet and don't eat the same menu every day, you need not be too concerned as to whether you are also getting enough vitamins and minerals. The chances are that you will be. A few words of advice. It's important not to overcook foods as this will destroy vitamins. Vitamins B and C

cannot be stored in the body. To ensure a good supply of these, for vit-
amin B eat some of the following every day: wholemeal bread and
cereals (white bread usually has vitamins and minerals added by the
miller but check labels), yeast extract, milk, cheese, eggs, lean meat
and green vegetables; for vitamin C eat fruit, especially citrus, green
vegetables, potatoes, salads and canned tomatoes.

Protein foods	Carbohydrate foods	Fats
Cheese (cottage and curd cheeses have the added advantage of being low in fat)	Fruit – fresh, dried and juice	Cheese
	Honey	Egg yolk
		Fish
Chicken and turkey	Pasta – especially wholemeal	Margarine – soft, such as soya, sunflower
Eggs – up to 5 a week	Pastries, biscuits, cakes, etc. made from wholemeal flour, oatmeal, nuts, dried fruit, vegetable oils – such as flapjacks, digestive biscuits, banana bread	
Fish		
Meat – lean		Meat
Milk		Milk
Nuts		Nuts
Pasta – especially wholemeal		Oils – poly-unsaturated
Peas – fresh or frozen	Peas – fresh or frozen	Poultry
Potatoes	Potatoes	Yogurt
Pulses – dried beans, peas, lentils, etc.	Pulses – dried beans, peas, lentils, etc.	
Rice – especially brown	Rice – especially brown	
Wholegrain cereals, oatmeal, etc.	Vegetables – fresh	
	Vegetables – dried, frozen and canned	
Wholemeal bread	Wholegrain cereals, oatmeal, etc.	
Wholemeal flour	Wholemeal bread	
Yogurt	Wholemeal flour	
	Yogurt	

Foods to be eaten less frequently

Bought biscuits, pies, cakes and puddings
Bought meat pies, sausage rolls, etc.
Canned meats and pies
Canned fruit
Fatty meat
Fats such as butter, lard, dripping and those margarines containing animal fats
Fizzy and sweetened drinks
Food fried in deep fat
Foods containing mono-sodium glutamate
High-fat cheeses and milk
Ice cream and cream
Potato crisps
Sliced and smoked ready-cooked meats
Smoked fish
Sugar, sugar coated cereals and sweets
White bread

If you eat plenty of fresh vegetables, wholemeal bread, pasta, rice and cereals, potatoes, nuts, fruit and pulses you will also be obtaining a good supply of fibre in your diet. This not only helps to make the digestive system work efficiently, it also helps to keep teeth and gums healthy by encouraging chewing.

Ideally we should eat three meals a day; this keeps us ticking over comfortably. You may prefer to eat lots of small snacks during the day. This doesn't matter as long as not too many of these snacks consist of foods best eaten less frequently. It is not a good idea to go for long stretches without any food at all. This causes headaches, drowsiness and lack of concentration. If you aim for the three-meals-a-day plan, you don't have to cook each time. Breakfast can be quite simple, consisting of fruit juice or a hot drink, and a bowl of cereal with perhaps some added fruit, nuts and yogurt; lunch might be at the canteen or could be sandwiches followed by some fruit; so the only meal you need actually cook would be in the evening and it doesn't have to be based on the concept of meat and two veg. You will find ideas for all sorts of different meals throughout the book. Basically every day you should make sure you eat some high-protein food such as fish, chicken, meat, cheese, eggs or pulses; eat plenty of food containing carbohydrates such as bread, cereals, potatoes, pasta or rice; eat as much fresh fruit and as many vegetables as you like.

SHOPPING AND STORING

Whether you shop every day or only two or three times a week is going to depend very much on your temperament, the time you have to spare and how much storage space is available. If you are not used to food shopping the huge variety of choice can be bewildering. Having made your choice it is not always easy to know how to store and keep it fresh. You may also be puzzled as to where is the best place in which to keep your food, both in terms of saving money and getting the freshest quality. The following notes are given to help you.

SHOPS

Supermarkets *Most large supermarkets are run extremely efficiently, so the food is likely to be fresh, competitively priced with just about everything you want under one roof. Once you are familiar with the layout, you can shop speedily, make your own choices and you will find that if you need help or advice it is usually readily obtainable. Their own brands are often good value and named brands are usually cheaper than other sources because the supermarkets can bulk-buy. Look out for bargains and reductions late on Saturday afternoons.*

Small shops *A small local shop which stays open late is handy, but expect to pay more for your goods as small shops often can't compete with supermarket prices. However, the owners are usually friendly and helpful and a good butcher, fishmonger or greengrocer is worth cultivating. They will advise you about what to buy, sometimes how to cook it, and a butcher or fishmonger will cut and bone items specially for you.*

Markets *Worth visiting, especially for local produce such as vegetables, fruit, fish, eggs, etc. Watch out for the odd bruised item that might be slipped in with the fresh things. Bargains are often to be had at the end of the day. Be especially careful about freshness if buying meat or fish.*

Wholefood shops, health shops and warehouses   *Often good value for buying grains, nuts, pulses, dried fruit, etc. Also for ready-mixed mueslis, nut butters, etc.*

FOODS

The following list is intended as a guide to some of the things you are likely to buy; it is not meant to be exhaustive. There are also some hints on how to store.

It is sensible to store all food covered. Uncovered food in a fridge becomes dehydrated and hard, and strongly flavoured foods will taint other food. Food left uncovered in a kitchen will attract flies and dirt, not to mention such delightful creatures as mice and possibly cockroaches. It is worth saving plastic bags, containers and jars with lids, and having a supply of cling film and foil.

PACKAGED, BAKED AND CANNED FOODS

Biscuits and cakes   *Should be kept in airtight containers. Don't mix the two as the biscuits will go soft.*
Bottled sauces   *Useful to have tomato ketchup (the Italian variety is good value), real mayonnaise, some supermarket own brands are good, salad cream; see also stock cubes and flavourings on page 30.*
Bread   *Can be kept wrapped in a fridge, or in a covered bread tin or, failing this, keep loosely wrapped in a plastic bag so that the air can circulate. Wholemeal bread contains all the natural nutrients of the wheat as well as more fibre than white bread. Wheatmeal bread is often made from white flour which has been coloured brown. This and white bread usually have had nutrients added by the miller but this is no longer statutory, so check your labels.*
Cans   *Handy to have one or two cans for when you don't have time to shop, such as tuna fish, sardines, soup, etc.*

Canned sauces are usually rather expensive. Cheaper and just as useful are condensed soups such as mushroom or chicken, which can be used, undiluted, as a sauce on things like pancakes, pasta, etc.

The best canned tomatoes are Italian, the sauce is thick and the flavour rich. Medium cans, about 400 g (13 oz), are often on special offer, so it is often much more economical to buy these rather than the smaller size. You can use half the can and store the rest in a covered container in the fridge for 3 or 4 days.

Coffee Fresh coffee loses flavour quickly, so buy in small quantities either freshly ground or in vacuum packs. Coffee buffs will want to buy the beans and grind their own. Coffee should be kept in an airtight container; it will keep longer if stored in a fridge, and it can be frozen. Instant coffee also has a short shelf-life, so only buy the large jars if you drink a lot. Freeze-dried instant coffee, although more expensive, is more like the real thing.

Flour Should be stored in an airtight container. Buy in small quantities unless you are doing a lot of baking. Storage time is about 3 months, after that watch out for weevils. Plain flour is the sort most often needed. If a recipe calls for self-raising flour, you can use plain flour but add a teaspoon of baking powder to every mug of flour. Cornflour is useful for making sauces. If making bread, ideally you should use 'strong' white flour and/or wholemeal flour.

Herbs and spices Will make and enhance your cooking. Dried herbs are readily obtainable and easily stored. Useful are thyme, oregano, parsley, bay leaves, sage and rosemary. Experiment with these and then try some of the others such as savory, dill, fennel, etc. The secret is to use them sparingly – dried herbs are much stronger than their fresh counterparts – and not combine more than two or three at a time. Useful spices are nutmeg, cinnamon, cumin, coriander, cloves, ginger, paprika.

Lemon juice The juice in plastic lemons or bottles is fine for flavouring.

Mixes Useful to have some on hand in the store cupboard such as bread, mashed potato, pizza base.

Oats, wheatflakes, nuts, wheatgerm, dried fruit For making up your own muesli. Keep in dry, covered containers.

Oils For cooking and for salads. Choose from corn, sunflower, safflower, soya or groundnut. These are all polyunsaturated. The cheaper oils labelled as cooking oils often have a slightly fishy taste and the money saved is minimal. For a treat, experiment with olive or walnut oils. Oils do not need to be refrigerated.

Pasta Useful to have some dried spaghetti and perhaps some pasta shells in store. Wholemeal pasta is good; it takes a little longer to cook.

Pulses Canned, such as lentils, chickpeas, baked and kidney beans. Pulses can also be bought dried, either in packets or loose.

Rice   *Use long-grain or Patna for boiled rice. Basmati is a delicious variety but more expensive. For risottos you will need the round-grain Italian variety, not the small-grain which is used for milk puddings. Brown rice contains more nutrients than white, the flavour is slightly nutty and it takes about twice as long to cook. Quick-cook rices are more expensive and once you've mastered the art of boiling rice, I think you'll agree they are not great savers of time or effort.*

Salt, pepper, mustard   *Salt needs to be kept dry; a few grains of rice added to it will keep it free-running.*

You can buy pepper in powder, white or black. Worth trying are the black peppercorns which you grind in a pepper mill; the flavour is infinitely more subtle and nearly all good cooks insist on using it.

Mustard can be bought powdered to be mixed as required with water, or you can buy it ready-mixed. Try the Dijon variety for a change from English, also experiment with the whole grain mustards.

Skimmed milk powder   *Use it to make up some milk in an emergency, make sauces or yogurt.*

Spreads   *Such as peanut butter, honey, yeast extract.*

Stock cubes and flavourings   *Various recipes list stock as an ingredient. This is the flavoured liquid which is obtained from boiling vegetables, chicken carcasses, etc. and there is a recipe on page 139. When you have no stock available, use a stock cube, a little yeast extract or a dash of Worcester sauce, mushroom ketchup or soya sauce mixed with water.*

Tea   *Loose tea is cheaper but tea bags are more convenient. Keeps well.*

Tomato purée   *Probably more useful and economical bought in tubes than in cans.*

Vinegar   *Best for salads are the wine or cider vinegars. Malt vinegar, though fine for pickling and sprinkling on fish and chips, is too strong for salad dressings.*

PERISHABLE AND FRESH FOODS

Bacon   *Keep wrapped in a fridge for up to 10 days. Eat within a day or two without a fridge. Streaky bacon is cheap but it has a high proportion of fat. Good buys are bacon pieces, and thin or very thin slices. Smoked bacon is quite salty, green or sweetcure bacon is mild.*

Cheese   *Keep wrapped in a cool place. Use hard varieties for cooking. Cottage cheese is low in fats. If you keep cheese in the fridge, take it out at least half an hour before using to develop its flavour. Dry, leftover cheese can be grated and will keep several days in an air-tight jar.*

Eggs *Are best cooked at room temperature, so they can be stored in the kitchen, but choose a cool place. If kept in the fridge, it's a good idea to take them out half an hour before cooking. They will keep up to 2 weeks in the kitchen, longer in the fridge.*

Fats for cooking and spreading *Sunflower margarines are more economical than butter and have a pleasant flavour. They have the added advantage of being polyunsaturated, and as they are soft they spread easily straight from the fridge. You can use cheaper hard margarines for spreading and cooking; and also for cooking there are the animal fats to choose from, such as lard or dripping. For making pastry you can use special white pastry fats. Fats will keep in the fridge for up to a month. If you have no fridge, it would be better to use oils for cooking and only buy small quantities of margarine or butter for spreading. In summer it might be worth buying an earthenware cooler, which can be obtained quite cheaply.*

Fruit *Keep in a cool place. You can use a fridge but it is not essential. Don't put bananas in a fridge because they will go black, or melons or pineapple as they will absorb the flavour of and taint other foods.*

Meat and fish *Need care in both storing and handling to avoid contamination from bacteria. Without a fridge, eat them the day you buy them. If storing in a fridge, fish should not be kept more than 24 hours and neither should mince or offal (liver, kidneys, etc.). Eat bought cooked meats within 2 days of purchase, also chicken and small cuts such as chops. A joint will keep for 3 or 4 days. Pre-packed meat or fish is often wrapped in tight-fitting plastic containers. It is necessary to let the air circulate a little around them, so loosen the fastenings, or remove and store in a plastic bag, tied with room to spare. Keep meat and fish near the top of the fridge, which is the coolest place, but make sure none of the juices can drip on to other foods, which might cause cross-infection. This especially applies to raw meat coming into close contact with already cooked meat.*

Once meat has been frozen, never refreeze it unless it has first been cooked. If you want to prepare meat ahead of time, say a casserole ready for a meal the following day, always cook it completely, let it cool down, then store in the fridge. Reheat to boiling point and then let it simmer for 15 or 20 minutes. Never partially cook meat in preparation for another meal. Always make sure that frozen meat is properly thawed, i.e. that no ice particles remain before you cook it. You can hasten the thawing of frozen meat by standing it under a running tap of cold water, never the hot tap. The reason for all these precautions is that bacteria can multiply rapidly in meat, especially under warm conditions.

How to choose meat: *It should be moist not wet, firm and elastic to touch and should have very little smell. Avoid butchers who do not keep meat in refrigerated counters or who in hot weather display meat in windows in full sun; also those who display cooked meats, sausages and bacon alongside raw meat.*

Beef should be dark red, with firm yellow fat.

Lamb should be dull red, with fat that is hard and white.

Pork should be pale pink, with fat that is soft and white.

Bacon should be pink, the fat white.

If you have any suspicion that meat is going off, if it has a strong smell or seems slightly slimy, throw it away. Salmonella poisoning is not funny.

How to choose fish: *Like meat, fish should be bought fresh. It should be firm, with hardly any smell, eyes bright, gills red. Ask the fishmonger to clean the fish for you, which means he will take out the innards, remove any spiky fins and descale it. Pre-wrapped fish is of course already cleaned, etc. Avoid a fishmonger who does not keep his fish under refrigerated conditions and one who allows flies free range.*

Milk *Light will destroy the vitamins in milk, so keep in the dark in a cool place. Again, in summer, an earthenware cooler could be useful. Silver top is the least fatty, or you can buy semi-skimmed or skimmed milk. Long-life or UHT milk is a good store standby and is often slightly cheaper than fresh milk, but it does have a distinctive flavour which is especially noticeable in tea. It is, however, extremely handy for making yogurt (see page 142).*

Vegetables *Best kept in a cool, dark place. You might be able to get a wooden, slatted box from your greengrocer. Eat green vegetables as soon as possible. Root vegetables will keep for about a week. Don't leave unrefrigerated in plastic bags as they will sweat and begin to ferment. Potatoes go green if kept in the light and become toxic. Keep salad vegetables loosely wrapped in plastic bags at the base of the fridge. If using only part of a vegetable which has a root, retain the root end until last; the vegetables will draw nourishment from it and stay fresh longer.*

Yogurt Will keep for several days in the fridge. Many commercial yogurts contain artificial sweeteners and flavourings, so it is worth settling for natural yogurt to which you can add your own flavourings, fruit, nuts, etc. Yogurt is simple to make (see page 142), and the cost is cut by at least half. Worth looking out for among commercial yogurts is the Greek variety, which is very thick and creamy and low in fat.

Part 2

ACTION

EASY BREAKFASTS

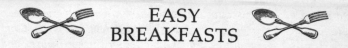

Breakfast is a good idea – it doesn't have to be very complicated and it need not be cooked. It can be simply a cup of tea or coffee or perhaps a glass of fruit juice with, say, a couple of pieces of toast. If you use wholemeal bread, so much the better. Or you could have half a grapefruit and a bowl of cereal. You might be lucky and have a canteen which provides a good breakfast, or you could grab some fruit and a carton of yogurt (don't forget that some bought yogurts are oversweetened; there's a recipe for home-made yogurt on page 142) and eat them when you get to college, supplemented by, say, a flapjack, or a slice of banana or peanut bread (recipes on pages 136–7).

If the limit of your achievement first thing in the morning is to be able to pour something into a glass and cut a slice off a loaf of bread, you might like to try one of the following.

ORANGE OR TOMATO JUICE WITH AN EGG

Break an egg into a glass, beat it with a fork, top up with juice, mix well. A dash of Worcester sauce goes well with tomato juice.

EGG FLIP

Make as above, but instead of fruit juice use milk and if you like sweeten it with a teaspoon of honey.

CEREALS

If you decide to have a bowl of cereal in the morning, you can make it more interesting by adding some slices of fruit – apples don't need peeling – or try it with dried fruit which will help to sweeten it – you may not need to add any sugar. Honey is pleasant instead of sugar and you only need a very little. As well as milk, try adding a dollop of yogurt.

From the point of view of food value, muesli is the best cereal choice.

You can buy it ready-mixed from health shops, supermarkets and food shops; 'own brands' are often cheaper. It is simple to mix your own and this way you will halve the cost. There are many variations on muesli and it is worth experimenting with different grains, fruit and nuts. It was originally invented by a Swiss, Dr Bircher-Benner, and intended as a light supper dish which formed a complete and nourishing meal. The original recipe calls for a large amount of fresh fruit to be eaten with the cereals and this is what makes it a really pleasant dish. Below is my own version.

MUESLI

> 4 mugs oatmeal
> 4 mugs wheatflakes
> 1 mug wheatgerm
> 1 mug chopped dried fruit
> 1 mug chopped nuts

Mix all the ingredients together and store in a covered container. At breakfast, put 2 tablespoons of the mixture into your bowl – or more or less to taste. Add sliced fruit such as an apple, a banana, 2 or 3 strawberries, a peach, an apricot, a pear, blackberries, raspberries, cherries, plums. Moisten with milk and add 2 or 3 tablespoons of yogurt.

COOKED BREAKFASTS

PORRIDGE

If you like the idea of something hot, you could make porridge. The instant variety is very easy and quick to make. Follow directions on the packet, which basically amounts to adding hot milk to the cereal. A pinch of nutmeg or cinnamon adds an interesting flavour.

If you like porridge and have it often you can make it from rolled oats or oatmeal and save a bit of money. Rolled oats are refined oatmeal and are often sold under the label 'porridge oats'; instructions are printed on the packets. If you buy rolled oats loose, the method is to allow three times as much water as oats (1 mug of water being about right for 1 serving). The water is brought to the boil, the oats sprinkled over and the mixture stirred thoroughly. It is then simmered for 4 or 5 minutes and stirred to prevent sticking. Because porridge burns easily, you must not skimp on the stirring. You can add salt if you like.

If you are using oatmeal, the cooking time is longer because it is much coarser than rolled oats. It will take about 20 minutes. You can shorten this time by soaking the oats in the measured amount of cold water overnight. Bring to the boil in the morning, stirring constantly, and then let the porridge simmer on a very low heat for 5–10 minutes.

BOILED EGG

If you can't stand porridge you could boil an egg. To prevent the shell cracking and white oozing all over the saucepan, try piercing a hole in one end with a needle. Remember that an egg straight from the fridge is likely to crack if put into boiling water. An egg can be boiled from cold, you start the timing when the water comes to the boil: 3½ minutes for a runny egg; 4 for a firm white and runny yolk; 5 for a firm yolk. Very fresh farm eggs need an extra ½ minute.

CODDLED EGG

Simpler than boiling is coddling. Half-fill a pan with water and bring it to the boil. Add the egg, remove the pan from the heat, cover, and leave for 5 minutes.

MUMBLED EGGS

An easy version of scrambled eggs which saves on the washing-up because the whole operation is done in the pan. Heat a frying pan over low heat and add a tablespoon of oil, margarine or butter. When it is foaming break in 1 or 2 eggs and stir quickly with a wooden spoon to mix them. Keep stirring until they are set but still moist. Add salt and pepper to taste.

BANANA AND BACON

A simple treat on a cold morning. Heat ½ tablespoon of oil, margarine or butter in a frying pan. Cut a peeled banana in half and wrap each half in a rasher of bacon. Fry gently until the bacon is crisp and the banana is soft, about 3–5 minutes.

THINGS ON TOAST

It doesn't matter what time of the day or night it is, something on toast could be the answer. If you have no grill or toaster then fry a piece of bread instead: make sure the pan is really hot, add a tablespoon of oil or fat, put in your bread and, as soon as it is golden, turn it and cook the other side. The hot pan will ensure the bread is not greasy.

Below are some ideas for things on toast.

CHEESE

Either grated or thinly sliced, set under the grill until it turns golden and bubbles. It's important not to overcook cheese or it will become stringy. Cheese can be added to a host of other things – a slice of ham, a sliced tomato, yeast extract, grilled bacon, sliced banana, bean-sprouts, sliced mushrooms. Simply top some lightly toasted bread with your chosen topping, add the cheese and put it under the grill. If you are using the grill to make your toast, economize by toasting one side only, then toast the other side with the topping.

WELSH RAREBIT

Mix ¼ teaspoon of mustard with 3 or 4 tablespoons of grated cheese, adding sufficient milk to form a thick paste. Spread it on the toast and set it under the grill until it is golden and bubbling.

BUCK RAREBIT

Make Welsh rarebit and top it with a poached egg (see next page). Try using a little beer instead of milk to mix the rarebit.

BEANS

Make one of the bean dishes on pages 72–73; and don't despise canned baked beans, they are great on their own or topped with an egg or sausage.

POACHED EGG

Half-fill a frying pan with water and bring it to the boil. Lower the heat. Pull the pan half-off the burner, so that only half the water is agitating. Break the egg on to a saucer and carefully slide it into the slightly bubbling water. By keeping half the water off the heat, the egg will form a good shape. Cover the pan and let the egg set, it will take about 4 minutes. If you find the water is bubbling fiercely, remove it completely from the heat. Poached eggs have a habit of becoming rather straggly – this is especially so if the egg is more than a few days old. Your first attempt may be disappointing but it is worth trying again, because once mastered, it's a handy way of cooking an egg.

As well as eating poached eggs on toast, with or without cheese, they are good accompaniments for spinach, or smoked fish such as haddock or kippers.

FRIED EGG

Heat a tablespoon of oil in a frying pan. When it is hot, break in the egg and let it cook over a medium heat. If you like the yolk covered with a cloudy skin, baste some of the hot oil over it while it is cooking.

SCRAMBLED EGGS

Heat a tablespoon of oil, margarine or butter in a frying pan or small saucepan over a low heat. Break 2 eggs into a bowl, beat with a fork until all the mixture is yellow, add a dessertspoonful of milk, and a pinch of salt and pepper. Mix. When the oil or fat is beginning to foam, pour in the eggs. Cook over a low heat. They will gradually thicken, as you gently stir them. They are ready when they are set and glistening. Don't cook beyond this point as they will become dry and leathery.

Scrambled eggs go well with grilled or fried tomatoes or mushrooms. You can stir in a tablespoon of grated cheese when the eggs are beginning to thicken. Or slice a courgette and cook it gently in oil or margarine for about 10 minutes and season it with salt and pepper and some mixed herbs before putting on top of the scrambled eggs.

MUSHROOMS

You'll need 75–100 g (3–4 oz). Wipe them with a piece of kitchen towel to remove any dirt. Leave whole, or quarter them if you prefer.

Either sprinkle with a little oil and grill under a medium heat until they are soft, 5–10 minutes; or heat a tablespoon of oil in a frying pan and fry the mushrooms over a medium heat for about 5 minutes.

TOMATOES

Allow 2 or 3 tomatoes. Cut them in half. Grill or fry them, skin side down first, turning them once, as for mushrooms. They will take a little less time.

SARDINES OR PILCHARDS

Either put them on the toast and heat under the grill for a couple of minutes; or mash them with a fork, add a few drops of Worcester sauce, lemon juice or vinegar and spread them on the toast. Try a little mustard spread on the toast before adding the fish and grilling.

SOFT HERRING ROES

Heat a tablespoon of oil or margarine in a small pan. When it is foaming add the roes. (To prevent them sticking to the pan, roll them in a little flour to coat them evenly.) Let them cook gently for 5–7 minutes, turning them once, until they are hot.

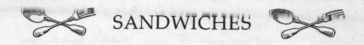

SANDWICHES

A sandwich is an extremely clever way of enclosing and keeping food fresh, as well as providing a simple but well-balanced meal. You can make conventional sandwiches using wholemeal or white sliced bread or you can experiment with all sorts of other breads. You can put fillings in rolls, pitta bread, baps, French sticks sliced lengthways or indeed any sort of bread base. Instead of using margarine or butter, you can ring the changes with mayonnaise, cream or curd cheese, cottage cheese, peanut or tahini butter (tahini butter is made from sesame seeds).

If you have access to a freezer, you can freeze-wrap sandwiches successfully; use plastic bags, cling film or foil (not paper). They defrost in 3–4 hours, so they will defrost by lunchtime if you take them out at breakfast time. If you do freeze sandwiches, avoid fillings with salad ingredients, salad creams or mayonnaise, hard-boiled eggs or bananas, as they don't freeze satisfactorily.

If you have a fridge, sandwiches will keep perfectly well overnight provided they are wrapped in plastic or foil rather than paper. To complete your lunch, you could have, say, a carton of fresh fruit juice or some milk; a piece of fruit; maybe a carton of yogurt, or some you have made yourself (see page 142). You'll probably already have your favourite sandwich fillings but here are some ideas to help you.

Sandwich fillings

Cheese with chutney, chopped dates, chopped nuts, tomato, cucumber, yeast extract, raisins, pineapple, sliced mushrooms, chopped peanuts – shelled fresh

Cottage cheese with tomato, sardine, banana, cucumber, chopped dates, chopped orange

Canned sweetcorn with mayonnaise, chutney

Banana with peanut butter, honey, ham, lemon juice, chocolate spread, honey and raisins, tahini butter

Peanut butter with honey, sardines, beansprouts, yeast extract, raisins

Scrambled or chopped hard-boiled egg (for how to hard-boil an egg
   see page 146) with peanut butter, lettuce, yeast extract
Grilled bacon – make the sandwich while the bacon is still warm
Sliced cold meat with tomato, lettuce, cucumber, pickle, mustard
Fish, such as sardines, pilchards, tuna, with cucumber, tomato,
   lettuce

TOASTED OR FRIED SANDWICHES

You don't have to have an electric sandwich-maker to prepare hot
sandwiches; you can make them by toasting or frying.

TOASTED SANDWICH

Toast two slices of bread on one side only. Put filling between the toasted sides, put back under the grill and toast the other two sides.

It's up to you whether you spread margarine or butter before putting in the filling.

FRIED SANDWICH

Heat your frying pan; spread two slices of bread with margarine or
butter, put in the first slice fat side down, add filling, top with second
slice fat side up. Turn the sandwich over when the bottom is golden
and cook the second side.

Or, simply make up your sandwich without adding any margarine
or butter to the filling; heat 2 tablespoons of oil or margarine in the
frying pan. When it is foaming, add the sandwich and cook as above.

FRIED SANDWICH WITH EGG AND MILK

Break an egg on to a plate or into a shallow dish; beat it with 2 tablespoons of milk. Heat 2 tablespoons of oil in a frying pan. Dip bread
into the egg mixture, put the first slice into the pan, add topping and
second slice of dipped bread. Cook until golden on both sides.

This is a good way of cheering up stale sandwiches if, say, you made
some for lunch and didn't get round to eating them.

Suggested fillings

Cheese, sliced or grated, cottage or curd either on its own or with
   sliced tomato, pickle, ham, mushrooms, beansprouts, sliced cold
   potato, yeast extract; try chopped orange with cottage cheese
Fish, such as sardines, pilchards, tuna, alone or with tomato
Baked beans
Meat such as leftover chicken, liver pâté, ham or Continental sausage,
   or corned beef
Grilled or fried bacon with banana or tomato
A fried egg
Mashed banana with lemon juice or honey
Sliced tomato with sweetcorn or peanut butter

There are ideas for sweet toasts and sandwiches on page 131.

OMELETTES

A whole mystique seems to surround the cooking of an omelette but really it is very simple provided you follow a few easy rules.

1. The frying pan must be absolutely clean otherwise the omelette will stick. This is why you will often hear that you should keep a special pan for omelettes. If you have a non-stick pan, it is easy to keep clean. If it does get encrusted with dirt, don't scour it with a metal pad or scouring powder, clean it instead with a good sprinkling of salt and a nylon brush.
2. The eggs must be beaten just before you are ready to cook them and only enough to incorporate the white with the yolk.
3. The omelette must be cooked quickly over high heat.

BASIC OMELETTE

1 tablespoon oil, margarine or butter
2 eggs
salt and pepper

Heat the frying pan over a medium heat. Beat the eggs until just mixed, and add a pinch of salt and some pepper. When the pan is hot add the oil, margarine or butter. Raise the heat and as soon as the oil or fat foams and splutters, pour in the egg mixture. Let it settle and begin to set. Lift the edges with a spatula, and tilt the pan so that the mixture runs underneath. Continue until the omelette is set but the top is still moist. Fold the omelette in half using the spatula, and slide it from the pan on to a plate.

You can eat omelettes absolutely plain or you can add all sorts of fillings or toppings. These can be added to the omelette just before you are ready to fold it over; or if there is a lot of filling, you can finish the cooking by putting the pan under a grill. Some fillings can be added raw, others must be cooked. If adding a cooked filling, you can save a little on the washing-up by cooking it first in your frying pan and then sliding it on to a plate; wipe the pan over with kitchen paper, then cook the eggs.

Ideas for fillings

Herbs   *Add ½ teaspoon of dried herbs or a teaspoon of chopped fresh herbs just before folding the omelette over. Try thyme, parsley, mixed herbs, oregano.*

Cheese   *Add 1 or 2 tablespoons of grated or cottage cheese just before folding the omelette over.*

Fish   *Chop some canned tuna, sardines or pilchards and add just before folding the omelette over.*

Cooked meat   *Chop a slice of cooked meat such as chicken, ham or corned beef, and add just before folding the omelette over.*

Potato   *Chop a cooked potato and add just before folding the omelette over. Or, peel and cut a raw potato into small dice, heat a tablespoon of oil in the frying pan and when it is hot, add the potato and cook over a medium heat until it is soft, 5–10 minutes. Remove from the pan, cook the omelette in the usual way, add the potato and fold the omelette over.*

Onion   *Chop an onion, heat a tablespoon of oil in the frying pan and when it is hot, add the onion and cook over a medium heat until it is soft and slightly brown, about 5 minutes. Remove from the pan, cook the omelette in the usual way, add the onion and fold the omelette over.*

Instead of, or as well as, an onion, you could use a chopped tomato, some sliced mushrooms, a chopped green pepper, a chopped rasher of bacon or slice of ham, a sliced courgette, a piece of bread cut into cubes, a tablespoon of sweetcorn or peas. Cook them in a tablespoon of hot oil until they are soft and hot through before proceeding with the omelette.

SPANISH OMELETTE

First cook some chopped onion in 2 tablespoons of oil, then add a variety of other chopped vegetables such as tomato, green pepper, cooked potato. Let them get hot for several minutes, pour over the egg mixture and let it set without stirring. When the base is golden brown, put the whole pan under a hot grill and cook until the top is set and beginning to brown.

PIPÉRADE

A dish from the Basque country. Chop an onion, cook it in hot oil in your frying pan until it is golden and soft, about 10 minutes. Add a thinly sliced green or red pepper. Cook for 5 minutes, stirring from time to time. Add a couple of chopped tomatoes, a little salt, pepper and oregano. Mix well. Lower the heat, cover the pan and let it cook for 5–10 minutes. Break the eggs into a bowl and beat to mix them. Pour over the vegetables, which should have become a soft purée, and stir gently until the eggs are set but the mixture is still moist.

POTATOES

The potato is cheap, it is easy to prepare and it will provide you with a very good base for a meal, as it contains protein as well as carbohydrates and some vitamins and minerals. The most effective way of preserving as much of its natural food value as well as flavour is to bake or boil it in its skin. The water can be used as an excellent base for soup or stock. It is rather extravagant to use the oven just to cook one potato but it is certainly worth while if there are several of you cooking together. You could always add some extra to be used as a base for an omelette, for example (see page 47), or for one of the dishes later in this section which use cooked potato. You can save fuel by boiling a potato in its skin and if you are adding a filling, you can put the potato in the oven or under the grill to heat the filling through and crispen the skin.

To prepare a potato for boiling or baking, scrub the potato under running water and cut out any damaged pieces. If cooking several, choose potatoes of uniform size – ask the greengrocer for ones which weigh about 275 g (10 oz) each.

TO BOIL A POTATO IN ITS SKIN

Half-fill a saucepan with water, bring it to the boil, and add your potato. Put on a lid and when the water returns to the boil, lower the heat and let it simmer until the potato is soft, 20–30 minutes.

TO BAKE A POTATO IN ITS SKIN

Prick the skin with a fork or cut one or two slits in the skin, this allows the steam to escape and prevents the potato bursting. If you like a crisp skin, put a very little oil in the palm of your hand and rub this over the potato. If you like a soft skin, you can wrap the potato in foil (the foil can be used more than once). Put the potato on a baking sheet near the top of the oven, set at Gas 6/400 °F/200 °C, for 50–60 minutes. It is possible to reduce the cooking time by spiking the potato on a potato baker, skewer or stainless steel fork, (see page 17). The metal acts as a heat conductor and will reduce the time by about 15 minutes.

The cooked potatoes can be eaten very simply by cutting in half and adding for example a little margarine or butter, cottage cheese, grated cheese, yogurt and some salt and pepper; or you can fill them with salad ingredients mixed with a little mayonnaise, salad dressing or yogurt.

STUFFED JACKET POTATOES

Cook the potato by one of the methods above. Cut it in half and using a teaspoon scoop out most of the flesh, leaving the skin intact. Mash the potato and mix it with your chosen filling – suggestions below – refill the potato halves, top them with a spoonful of grated, cottage or curd cheese and return them to the oven for 5–10 minutes, or put under a hot grill until the cheese is melted.

Suggested fillings

Two or three chopped mushrooms with a spoonful of yogurt
A chopped, fried bacon rasher with a tablespoon of leftover vegetables such as cabbage, carrots, Brussels sprouts or peas
A slice of ham, chopped, mixed with a little mustard
A tablespoon of tuna, sardines or pilchards, moistened with a tablespoon of tomato ketchup
A beaten egg
A tablespoon of leftover chicken, moistened with yogurt or milk
An onion, chopped and fried
A tablespoon of cottage cheese with a diced tomato
A tablespoon of sweetcorn or baked beans
A tablespoon of grated cheese with a tablespoon of pickle

EGG COOKED IN POTATO

Cook the potato by one of the methods above. Take off a slice across the top of the potato and hollow out sufficient potato to take an egg. Break the egg into the hollow and return to the oven until the egg is set, about 10 minutes. (Save the leftover potato for another dish, see ideas below.)

Some dishes using cooked potato

The simplest way to use cooked potato is to fry it and perhaps eat it with some cold meat, or you could use it as a base for an omelette, in soup, or in the filling of a toasted sandwich.

FRIED POTATO

Heat about 2 tablespoons of oil or cooking fat in a frying pan. When it is foaming add the sliced potato, no need to peel; cook over a medium heat until brown, turn and cook the other side – it will take 5–10 minutes. Season with salt and pepper.

Below are a couple of more substantial ideas; you could make more of a meal by adding a fried egg, a couple of sausages or some cold meat.

BUBBLE AND SQUEAK

   1 tablespoon oil or cooking fat
   about 3–4 tablespoons cooked greens
   the same quantity of chopped or mashed cooked potato
   salt and pepper
   pinch of nutmeg

Heat the oil or fat in a frying pan until it just begins to foam. Cut the greens into small pieces, add to the pan with the potato, mix and press well down to cover the base of the pan. Add a pinch of salt, some pepper and the nutmeg. Cook the bubble and squeak over a medium heat until the bottom is crisp and brown, about 5–10 minutes.

POTATO AND BACON WITH CHEESE

   1 tablespoon oil or cooking fat
   1 onion, chopped
   2 rashers streaky bacon
   1 cooked potato
   salt and pepper
   1 small green pepper (optional)
   1 tomato
   3 tablespoons grated cheese

Heat the oil or fat in a frying pan. When it is just beginning to foam add the chopped onion. Cut the bacon into small pieces and add, cook until the onion is soft – about 5 minutes. Slice the potato and add. Cut the pepper, if using, into small pieces, discarding the seeds, and add. Cook over a medium heat, stirring frequently, until it is heated throughout – about 5 minutes. Add a pinch of salt and some pepper. Heat the grill. Slice the tomato, lay on top of the mixture, scatter the grated cheese over and grill until the cheese is golden and melted. (Do be careful, if your frying pan has a wooden or plastic handle, not to let the handle get under the grill.)

MASHED POTATO

Use potatoes baked or boiled in their skins. The skin will come away very thinly if you peel them while they are still warm. Or use leftover potato. Mash the potatoes using a fork, a potato masher or even a milk bottle to remove all the lumps. (If you have a Mouli-légumes (see page 16) you will find it extremely useful for this purpose.) Mix about a tablespoon of margarine or butter with the hot potato, add enough milk to form a thick purée and season with a pinch of salt and pepper. Instant mash: Dried potato mixes are a useful standby. They are more expensive than fresh but great timesavers.

Mashed potato can be fried, in which case after you have heated the oil or fat in the frying pan, press the potato well down into the pan, fry until the underneath is crisp and golden and carefully turn it over, using two spatulas if necessary. Fry until the base is golden, 5–10 minutes on each side.

HASH WITH POTATO AND COOKED MEAT

> 1 tablespoon oil or cooking fat
> 1 onion, chopped
> 50 g (2 oz) cooked meat (ham, corned beef, chicken, etc.),
>   chopped – about 2 tablespoons
> 4 tablespoons mashed potato
> ¼ teaspoon thyme or mixed herbs
> salt and pepper, to taste

Heat the oil or fat in a frying pan. When it is hot add the chopped onion. Cook until it is soft, about 5 minutes. Mix the meat with the potato and add to the pan with the herbs. Press the mixture well down to cover the base of the pan. Cook over a medium heat until the base is golden brown, about 5 minutes. Turn the hash over and cook the other side. You may find it easier to turn if you invert a plate over the pan, turn the whole thing over so that the hash falls on to the plate and then slide the hash back into the pan. Cook until the underside is crisp and golden, taste, and add salt and pepper if necessary. If you find it difficult to turn, brown the second side under a hot grill.

FISH HASH

Prepare as above but substitute fish for the meat. You can use any leftover cooked fish, or sardines, pilchards, tuna, etc.

# PIZZAS

The most familiar base for a pizza is made of a bread dough. You will find a recipe for this on page 141. It is easy to make but you have to allow sufficient time for the dough to rise, so you will probably feel this is only worth making if you are planning to feed some friends and are making one or two large pizzas.

There are a variety of other bases that you can use. Quickest of all are ready-made bases such as split muffins or crumpets, pitta bread, French bread sliced lengthways, or even toast. To all these you simply add your topping and put them under a hot grill or in the oven for a few minutes.

If you want a more substantial meal you can make a scone base (see page 55), which can be cooked in the oven or in the frying pan but, as there is no yeast involved, needs no rising time. Or you can make a base using a potato pastry which is especially good if cooked in a frying pan. In a great deal of hurry, use a pizza base mix or a scone mix; or in less of a hurry, a bread mix – it is easier than making dough from scratch but you must allow a little extra time for the dough to rise. Directions for making up and cooking will be on the packets.

BASIC PIZZA TOPPING

This consists of a layer of tomatoes, which can be fresh, sliced tomatoes or drained and crushed canned tomatoes or Italian tomato or pizza sauce spread over the base. If you like garlic, add a clove cut in tiny dice or crushed, with a pinch of salt and pepper and ¼ teaspoon per person of dried oregano or basil or marjoram (if fresh herbs are obtainable, chop them and add twice as much). Cover with a layer of cheese, either grated or thinly sliced. Mozzarella or Parmesan are delicious but costly, so instead use a hard English cheese or a curd cheese.

You can cook your pizza with just the above topping or you can add other things. The amount you add will depend on size of base and hunger.

Additions to basic pizza topping

Sliced mushrooms

Ham, salami, garlic sausage, mortadella, etc., cut in strips

Sardines, anchovy fillets, pilchards, tuna

Red or green pepper, thinly sliced

Frankfurter or other smoked sausage, cut in thin rings

Cooked ordinary sausage, cut in rings

Courgette or aubergine, cut in rings and cooked gently until soft in a little oil

A few green or black olives

Finely sliced onion, cooked until soft in a little oil, allow 10–15 minutes

Sweetcorn

Mussels, try those tinned in brine rather than vinegar

A few shelled prawns or shrimps

You can ring the changes to suit yourself, but it is probably wise not to add a huge variety of different things, as their tastes will cancel each other out.

SCONE BASE *for oven or frying pan (1 or 2 servings)*

> 1 mug plain flour (or ½ plain and ½ wholemeal if you wish)
> 1 teaspoon baking powder (or use self-raising flour and omit baking powder)
> pinch of salt
> 1 tablespoon oil
> 2–3 tablespoons water

Sieve the flour, salt and baking powder into a bowl (if using wholemeal flour, the coarse grains will remain in the base of the sieve, add these when all the flour has gone through). Make a hollow in the middle, add the oil and 1 tablespoon of water. Using a knife, mix, adding more water as you need it to make a firm and spongy dough. Put some flour on your hands – to prevent the dough sticking to them – and form the dough into a ball. Sprinkle about a tablespoon of flour on to a board or flat surface, and roll the dough into a circle to fit your frying pan; or if baking, roll to a diameter of about 20 cm (8 inches).

To cook in the oven   *Heat the oven to Gas 7/425 °F/220 °C. Place pizza on a baking sheet which you have smeared with oil. Dabble a little oil – about a tablespoon – over the base before adding the topping. Cook for about 30 minutes until the cheese is melted and golden and the base is cooked through.*

To cook in a frying pan   *Heat a tablespoon of oil in the frying pan and add the dough. Cook the scone base over a medium heat for about 5 minutes until the underside is golden, turn it over and add the topping. Cover the pan, lower the heat and cook until the base is golden, the cheese has melted and it is heated throughout – about 15 minutes. You can brown the top under a hot grill for 2 or 3 minutes if you wish.*

POTATO BASE   *for oven or frying pan (1 or 2 servings)*

> ½ mug mashed potato
> salt and pepper
> 1 tablespoon oil or melted margarine
> 3 tablespoons plain flour
> ¼ teaspoon baking powder
> 1–2 teaspoons water or milk

Using a knife, mix the mashed potato with a pinch of salt, some pepper and the oil or margarine. Add the flour and baking powder. Add the water or milk to form a dough. Sprinkle about a tablespoon of flour on to the board and roll the dough into a circle to fit your frying pan; or if baking, roll to a diameter of about 20 cm (8 inches).

Cook in the oven, as above. Or, to cook in a frying pan, put the potato base into the frying pan, add the topping, cover and fry over a moderate heat until the base is golden. Check that the base is not getting too brown before the top is cooked, if necessary lower the heat. Brown under a hot grill for 2 or 3 minutes if you wish.

READY-COOKED BASES

Cook bases such as muffins, bread, ready-cooked pizza base, etc. under the grill. Make sure the grill is hot – heat it for 5 minutes – add the topping and grill until the cheese is melted.

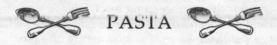# PASTA

Pasta comes in a variety of different shapes, it is very quick and easy to cook and with the addition of a simple sauce and perhaps some grated cheese, will provide you with a highly nutritious meal. The Italians have a variety of traditional uses for the different shapes and sizes. Fortunately, rules are made to be broken, so I suggest you begin by buying, say, long spaghetti and perhaps one of the shell shapes, try some of the suggested sauces and then go on to discover other books which enlarge on the delights of this type of cooking.

Pasta is most readily obtainable dried and as it keeps well is probably most useful for your purpose. More and more shops are selling freshly made pasta; it does take only a few minutes to cook but as it is rather expensive, I suggest to begin with you keep to the dried. You can buy white and wholemeal pasta; the second takes a few extra minutes to cook but the flavour is very good, and it contains more nutrients.

TO COOK PASTA

Allow 75–100 g (3–4 oz) per person, estimate the quantity by the weight of the package.

1. Use a large pan, allow 1.7 litres (3 pints) of water for every 225 g (8 oz) pasta.
2. Bring the water to the boil, add ½ teaspoon of salt and 1 teaspoon of oil. The oil will stop the water boiling over.
3. Keep the water boiling as you add the pasta, add it gradually, letting long spaghetti coil itself into the pan.
4. Let it boil briskly, uncovered. Stir it with a fork from time to time to make sure it is not sticking to the base.
5. Follow cooking times on packet, this will be somewhere between 6 and 15 minutes depending on the shape of the pasta.

6. Test by taking out a piece and biting it, it should be soft but very slightly chewy, not mushy.
7. Drain it thoroughly using a colander or sieve.
8. Heat a tablespoon or two of oil, margarine or butter in the pan and when it is hot, return the pasta, toss it with a fork to coat each piece, and add some pepper. If you have a pepper mill so much the better.

(If you have any pasta left over, you can use it as a base for a salad, or it can be reheated by covering with boiling water and immediately draining.)

SAUCES FOR PASTA

While the pasta is cooking, prepare your sauce. Quantities are for 1 person.

Butter and cheese *Simply toss the pasta in 2 tablespoons of melted butter and sprinkle some grated cheese over it.*

Cheese and egg *Prepare as above, break an egg into the pasta and mix quickly to coat the pasta with the mixture.*

Bacon and onion *Heat frying pan and when it is hot, add a couple of rashers of bacon cut in small pieces. When the fat runs out, add a chopped onion. Let it cook for 5–10 minutes. Mix with the pasta and top with grated cheese.*

Chickpeas *Heat the contents of half a can of chickpeas (or use 2 or 3 tablespoons of chickpeas you have cooked yourself – see pages 71–2). Drain and mix with the cooked pasta and top with grated cheese.*

Onion with mushroom *Heat a tablespoon of oil in a frying pan. Add a chopped onion, cook until soft – about 5 minutes. Add 3 or 4 sliced mushrooms and a pinch of herbs such as thyme or marjoram. Cook until the mushrooms are soft (3 or 4 minutes), season to taste with salt and pepper. Mix with the pasta.*

Onion with tuna or sardines or pilchards *Prepare as for onion with mushroom, substituting the contents of a small can of tuna or sardines or pilchards for the mushrooms. (You can use the oil from the can to cook the onion.)*

Onion with ham, salami, garlic sausage, etc. *Prepare as for onion with mushroom, substituting a slice of cooked meat for the mushrooms.*

BASIC TOMATO SAUCE   (2 servings)

There are a whole number of sauces based on tomato. To make a basic
Italian tomato sauce you do need really well-flavoured tomatoes. The
Italians understand this very well so, except for a short time in the
summer when tomatoes are good and cheap, I suggest you buy Italian
canned tomatoes. The cans come in three sizes. The medium tin, about
400 g (14 oz), is very often on special offer and is not much more expensive than the small one. I therefore suggest you use this size to
make your tomato sauce, using half for one meal and setting the other
half aside in a covered container to use another time. The sauce will
keep for several days in the fridge.

1 tablespoon oil or cooking fat
1 onion, chopped
1 clove of garlic, chopped (optional)
1 tablespoon tomato purée
1 teaspoon sugar
½ teaspoon dried oregano, marjoram or basil
medium can Italian tomatoes or 225 g (8 oz) fresh
    tomatoes, sliced
salt and pepper

Heat the oil or fat in a small saucepan. When it is hot, add the chopped
onion and let it cook gently for about 5 minutes. Add the other ingredients with a pinch of salt and some pepper. Bring to the boil,
cover, lower heat and let it simmer for 15–20 minutes.

You can eat this sauce with your pasta with perhaps the addition of
some grated cheese. It can also have other things added to it and below
are some suggestions.

Suggested additions

Canned fish   When the basic sauce is cooked, add the contents of a
can of sardines, pilchards, tuna, mussels or prawns – you could use a
tablespoon of the oil from the can to soften the onion; discard the rest.
Let the sauce heat through for 3 or 4 minutes.
Sweetcorn, chickpeas, or other pulses   When the basic sauce is
cooked, add the contents of a can of sweetcorn or chickpeas, or other
pulses such as haricot beans, kidney beans, etc.; or use some of your

*own cooked pulses – see pages 71–2 for cooking methods. Heat the
sauce through for 3 or 4 minutes.*

*Other additions will need longer cooking time than the preceding two
ideas. Cook your onion as in the basic tomato sauce, then add one of
the following. Let it cook for 2 or 3 minutes, then proceed with the
recipe.*

Green pepper, chopped, seeds discarded
Ham and mushrooms, chopped
Bacon, chopped
Courgettes or aubergine, sliced
Mushrooms, sliced
*Mince or chicken livers, allow 100 g (4 oz) per serving. Discard any
    green bits in the livers, which cause a bitter flavour.*

LASAGNE OR CANNELLONI   *(for 4 and upwards)*

*More elaborate pasta dishes can be made by layering pasta, a meat
sauce, and cheese or a cheese sauce. They do take a certain amount of
time to prepare but are a marvellous way of feeding lots of people well
and reasonably cheaply. Because of the time needed to prepare them,
don't decide to do them half an hour before you want to eat. You will
end up feeling frantic and wishing you had never begun.*
    The dishes are made up as follows:
*Pasta – flat sheets of lasagne or tubes of cannelloni are the most usual
pasta for these dishes but you can use shell or other shapes.*
A sauce – which consists of a basic tomato sauce with meat.
A cheese sauce or sliced or grated cheese.
The method is as follows:

1. Cook pasta as described on page 57. For 4 people,
   allow 225–350 g (8–12 oz) depending on appetites.
   Drain it. To save time and effort you can use pre-
   cooked or ready-cooked pasta instead.
2. Make a sauce following the instructions for a basic
   tomato sauce on page 59. At the stage where the
   onions are cooked, add 450 g (1 lb) mince and let it
   brown for 3 or 4 minutes, stirring; continue with the
   basic recipe.
3. Make a cheese sauce, see page 139, doubling quan-

tities. Or you can decide to omit this sauce and top
the dish with grated or sliced cheese; allow 75–100 g
(3–4 oz).

4. To assemble, smear a little oil over a shallow oven
dish. Put in layers of meat sauce, pasta and cheese
sauce, finishing with a layer of cheese sauce. Sprinkle
1 or 2 tablespoons of grated cheese over the top. *Or*,
layer meat sauce and pasta, finishing with a layer of
meat sauce, and top with sliced or grated cheese. *Or*, if
using cannelloni, fill the tubes with the meat sauce
mixture using a teaspoon, lay the filled tubes in the
dish and pour over the cheese sauce. Top with a tablespoon or two of grated cheese.

5. Bake at Gas 4/350 °F/180 °C for 45 minutes until the top
is golden brown. If using sliced or grated cheese, it is a
good idea to cover the dish with foil for the first 20 minutes of cooking time as otherwise the cheese may
brown too quickly. If using pre-cooked dried pasta,
allow an extra 5–10 minutes cooking time, and a little
more liquid, see instructions on packet.

*This dish can be assembled ahead of time. Let it cool before putting it,
covered, into the fridge. Allow an extra 20–30 minutes cooking time
to make sure it is hot through. If using an earthenware dish, put it
into a cold oven because going from the fridge straight into a hot oven
might crack it. Allow an extra 30–40 minutes cooking time.*

SPAGHETTI BOLOGNESE

*If you feel this all sounds like too much trouble but you want to feed a
group of friends give them spaghetti bolognese.*

*Prepare a basic tomato sauce as on page 59. When the onion is soft,
add 75 or 100 g (3 or 4 oz) mince per person and let it brown. Add
some sliced mushrooms, 25–50 g (1–2 oz) per person, and a chopped
green pepper. Let them cook a few minutes and then proceed with the
basic recipe, if necessary using a large can of tomatoes.*

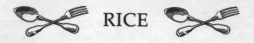# RICE

Rice is a useful base for many dishes. It is perhaps as well to remember that the white variety has been refined to such an extent that it has lost a good deal of its nutrients. So it wouldn't be wise to limit yourself to a daily diet of rice and little else. If you have a passion for rice, it would be well worth while buying the brown variety which hasn't been subjected to the same refining processes. It does take longer to cook but has an extremely pleasant nutty flavour.

When buying white rice to boil, choose the long-grain kinds such as Patna or more expensively Basmati. Risotto calls for short-grain Italian rice (see notes on page 30).

BOILED RICE

> 1 mug water
> pinch of salt
> ½ mug rice

Boil the water in a saucepan, add the salt and rice. Reduce the heat to lowest possible setting, cover the pan and simmer for 20 minutes. Turn off the heat and leave 5–10 minutes, without lifting lid.

RICE PILAFF

> 1 tablespoon oil
> 1 small onion, chopped
> ½ mug rice
> 1 mug water or stock (if you have no stock you could flavour the water with ¼ teaspoon marmite or 1 teaspoon of mushroom ketchup)

Heat the oil in a saucepan. When it is hot, add the chopped onion and let it soften for 3 or 4 minutes; add the rice, stir it until every grain is glistening with oil. Add the water or stock and bring to the boil. Cover the pan, simmer on lowest heat for 20 minutes. Turn off heat and leave 5–10 minutes without lifting lid. (If you have used water, you may need to add a little salt.)

BROWN RICE

½ mug brown rice
1 mug water
1 tablespoon oil, margarine or butter
pinch of salt

Put all the ingredients into a saucepan. Bring it to the boil, then lower the heat, cover, and simmer on lowest heat for 30–40 minutes. Leave covered for 10 minutes before serving.

If you find that your rice is sticky and the grains are not separate, put it into a colander and pour boiling water over it; this will wash out some of the starch. Stir cooked rice with a fork as this helps to keep the grains separate, a spoon will tend to make it mushy. Many of the sauces given in the pasta chapter (page 58) go well with rice.

USING COOKED RICE

Rice can be used as a base for salads, in which case mix with your chosen dressing while it is still warm (see page 123). If you have some leftover rice it can be used as a base for a very satisfying meal. You will need about 1 mug of cooked rice per person.

SIMPLE FRIED RICE

Heat some oil, margarine or butter in a frying pan, add the cooked rice, stir it with a wooden fork and let it heat until it is piping hot. Season with salt and pepper and, if you like, break in an egg and mix it quickly to coat the rice all over.

TASTY FRIED RICE

Heat some oil, margarine or butter in a frying pan, add a chopped onion and a piece of bacon, cut into small pieces. Cook over a high heat, stirring all the time, then push to one side and add a tablespoon of oil, break in an egg, stir it and let it begin to set. Add the rice and 2 or 3 tablespoons of frozen peas. Mix well and add a few drops of soy sauce. Let it cook over a low heat for several minutes, until it is piping hot.

You can add other ingredients to this basic recipe including cooked chicken or meat cut into small pieces, chopped green pepper, chopped tomato, finely sliced mushrooms, finely sliced vegetables or minced meat. If you have a wok it is, of course, ideal for this type of quick fried cooking. The secret is to cook all the other ingredients quickly over high heat, stirring constantly, then add the rice and seasoning. If it seems a little dry, moisten with stock made with a cube, or use vegetable water. If using raw minced meat, let it cook over a lower heat for 5–10 minutes after the initial quick frying before adding the egg and the other ingredients.

RISOTTO

In order to make a good risotto it is essential to use short-grain Italian rice. Unlike pilaff where the rice is dry, in this type of dish the rice is rich and creamy. It is best to use a well-flavoured stock which can be made from a chicken carcass (see page 139) or from a chicken stock cube.

The stock is added to the pan gradually as the rice absorbs the liquid, so it is a dish that needs to be tended carefully and is something that is probably best made when you are cooking for more than one person.

BASIC RISOTTO   *(4 servings)*

   4 mugs stock
   3 tablespoons oil
   1 onion, chopped
   1 clove of garlic, crushed
   225 g (8 oz) mushrooms, sliced
   1½ mugs Italian rice
   4 tablespoons butter
   3–4 tablespoons grated cheese
   salt and pepper

Boil the stock and keep it hot. In a large saucepan heat the oil and fry the onion. After a few minutes add the crushed garlic and sliced mushrooms. Cook for several minutes, stirring. Add the rice and mix so that every grain is coated with oil. Add about a third of the stock, stir well and let it simmer. Gradually add the rest of the stock, stirring all the time, until it is all absorbed. The whole process should take 20–25 minutes, by which time the rice should be thick and creamy. Take care that it does not stick. Stir in the butter, season with salt and pepper and serve with the cheese either mixed in or sprinkled on top.

Suggested additions

Fry 225 g (8 oz) chicken livers in a little oil or butter until they are well-browned. Remove from the frying pan and follow the above recipe. When the rice has been added and mixed, add a tablespoon of tomato purée and the livers and continue as above.

Instead of mushrooms use sliced courgettes, broccoli, tomato, asparagus tips, chopped celery, chopped cooked chicken or ham.

To use leftover risotto, heat a tablespoon of oil, margarine or butter in a frying pan. Add 2 or 3 tablespoons of risotto, press down well. Cook over a low heat until the base is golden; turn by inverting it on to a plate, melt more oil or butter and cook the other side until it is brown.

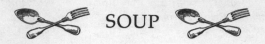# SOUP

Soup is easy to make and a relatively cheap way of providing you with a splendid meal, especially if you eat it with a good hunk of bread and perhaps a sprinkling of grated cheese over the top. To make it more filling you can add a tablespoon or two of pasta, rice or lentils (which don't need soaking, see page 71).

Basically you need a few vegetables, which are cooked for a few minutes in a little oil, margarine or butter, and liquid in some form: either water flavoured with a stock cube; a stock which is the liquid made from cooking meat bones; or the water in which vegetables have been cooked (potato water is especially good and nutritious); or a mixture of stock and milk. There is a recipe for making your own stock on page 139.

It really isn't worth making only sufficient soup for 1 serving. Soup can be kept for several days in the fridge; if you haven't one, it is important to bring the soup to boiling point every 24 hours, otherwise it will begin to ferment.

I have chosen soup ideas which can be eaten just as they are but if you like soups which are puréed most of them will adapt well to this method. If you have a sieve you can push the cooked ingredients through this, mixing them with the liquid in which they were cooked. This can be a tedious business, so if you like soup purées, it would be well worth buying a Mouli-légumes, see page 16. This is much cheaper than a liquidizer and has many uses in the kitchen.

BASIC VEGETABLE SOUP *(3 or 4 servings)*

> 1–2 tablespoons oil, margarine or butter
> 1 onion, chopped
> 450 g (1 lb) chosen vegetable
> 3 mugs stock or water
> salt and pepper

Heat the oil in a saucepan, and when it is hot add the chopped onion.

Let it soften for 3 or 4 minutes. Clean and chop the other vegetables into small pieces and add to the pan. Mix well, put on the lid and leave over a gentle heat for about 10 minutes. (This process is called 'sweating', and means that the vegetables will exude their flavour and make the resulting soup more tasty.) Pour over the stock or water, add a pinch of salt and some pepper and bring to the boil. Cover, lower the heat and let the soup simmer for about 30 minutes.

Details about preparing different vegetables are on page 112. If you are not able to purée or liquidize your soup, the vegetables are more attractive if they are cut quite small. Since you are eating vegetables and liquid, you will still be getting all their goodness.

You can make the flavour of vegetable soups more interesting by adding herbs such as basil, parsley, tarragon, chives, chervil or mint. It's best to use one herb at a time so that you can enjoy its particular flavour. Allow ½ teaspoon dried herbs, twice as much if using fresh.

To thicken soups: you can thicken soups by mashing 1 mug of the cooked vegetables and returning this purée to the pan; alternatively stir in 1 or 2 tablespoons of instant mashed potato; or mix 1 tablespoon of cornflour with 2 or 3 tablespoons of cold water and a little of the hot soup. Stir this paste into the soup off the heat – it will go lumpy if added to boiling liquid.

Vegetables to use

Leek and potato   Use equal quantities of each.

Carrot and potato   Use equal quantities of each.

Spinach or watercress with leek and potato   225 g (8 oz) spinach or a bunch of watercress, 2 leeks and 2 potatoes. (The spinach needs to be washed in several changes of water as it tends to be gritty.) When the soup is cooked add ½ mug of milk or a spoonful or two of yogurt. A pinch of nutmeg goes well with spinach; add it with the salt and pepper.

Leek, tomato and pepper   2 leeks and a red or green pepper (remove seeds), sweated with the onion. Add a couple of chopped tomatoes and a teaspoon of basil or oregano.

Carrot, onion and pea   225 g (8 oz) carrots, a bunch of spring onions or a large onion and 100 g (4 oz) peas. (You can use frozen peas, in which case add them 5 minutes before the end of cooking time.)

ITALIAN VEGETABLE SOUP   *(3 or 4 servings)*

Cut a couple of rashers of bacon into small pieces and cook with the onion, as in basic vegetable soup, above. Add a combination of vegetables such as carrots, potatoes, leeks, a few cabbage leaves or celery. After the vegetables have sweated add a medium can of Italian tomatoes, 3 tablespoons of rice or small pasta – if using spaghetti, break it into pieces about 2.5 cm (1 inch) long – and the stock. Serve with grated cheese.

FRENCH ONION SOUP   *(3 or 4 servings)*

> 900 g (2 lb) onions
> 2 tablespoons oil, cooking fat or butter
> 1 teaspoon sugar
> 3 mugs stock (made with a beef stock cube)
> salt and pepper
> slices of cheese
> toast

Peel and slice the onions. Heat the oil or fat in a pan and add the onions and the sugar (the sugar will help the onions to brown). Cook the onions over a medium heat until they are soft and brown, about 10–15 minutes, turning them occasionally. Pour in the stock, bring to the boil, lower heat and simmer for 15 minutes. Season to taste with salt and pepper. Put slices of cheese on the toast, and brown the cheese under the grill. Float a piece of toasted cheese on top of each bowl of soup.

BEETROOT SOUP – BORTSCH   *(3 or 4 servings)*

> 1 onion
> 450 g (1 lb) uncooked beetroot (beetroot is usually sold cooked, so ask for an uncooked one)
> 1 carrot
> 1 small parsnip
> 3 mugs water or stock
> 225 g (8 oz) cabbage
> 1 teaspoon sugar
> salt and pepper
> 1 heaped tablespoon tomato purée
> natural yogurt

Peel and cut the onion, beetroot, carrot and parsnip into thin pieces, about 5 cm (2 inches) long. Put in a saucepan and add the stock. Bring to the boil, lower the heat and cover and simmer for 30 minutes. Cut the cabbage into fine strips and add. Cook uncovered for 15 minutes. Add the sugar and season to taste with salt and pepper. Stir in the tomato purée and simmer for a further 10 minutes. Serve topped with a spoonful of yogurt in each bowl.

SWEETCORN SOUP *(3 or 4 servings)*

1 tablespoon oil, cooking fat or butter
1 onion, chopped
2 potatoes, chopped
1 tablespoon plain flour
1 mug water or stock
1 pint milk
salt and pepper
Medium can of sweetcorn

Heat the oil or fat, add the chopped onion and potato and cook covered for 5–10 minutes. Stir in the flour. Gradually add the water or stock and milk. Season to taste with salt and pepper. Bring to the boil, stirring to prevent lumps forming. Add the sweetcorn. Cook for 20 minutes over a low heat.

SCOTCH BROTH *(4 servings)*

This is a filling meal, using meat and vegetables.

450 g (1 lb) scrag end of lamb, cut in portions
450 g (1 lb) mixed vegetables, such as carrot, onion, turnip, leek, potato
4 mugs stock or water
3 tablespoons pearl barley
salt and pepper

Put the meat into a pan, peel and cut the vegetables into small pieces and add. Pour over the stock or water and bring to the boil. Skim off with a spoon any scum that has come to the top and add the pearl barley. Cover the pan, lower the heat and simmer for 2 hours. As lamb from the scrag end has a high proportion of fat, this soup is best cooked the day before you wish to eat it. Allow it to get cold, then

*refrigerate. Next day remove the layer of fat on the surface. Season
with salt and pepper, bring the soup to the boil over a high heat, lower
the heat, cover the pan and let it simmer 10–15 minutes before serving.*

FISH SOUP *(3 or 4 servings)*

> 2 leeks
> 2 potatoes
> 2 carrots
> 1 tablespoon oil, cooking fat or butter
> ¼ teaspoon nutmeg
> 3 mugs stock or water
> salt and pepper
> 450 g (1 lb) cod or other white fish fillet

*Prepare the vegetables; cut the leeks into rings, chop the potatoes and
carrot. Heat the oil or fat in a saucepan and cook the vegetables with a
lid on for about 10 minutes. Add the nutmeg and stock or water,
season to taste with salt and pepper. Bring to the boil, cover, lower
heat and cook for 10 minutes. Add the fish, cut in small pieces. Cook
for 10 minutes.*

*Tomatoes go well with fish, so you could add a can of Italian
tomatoes, or stir in a tablespoon of tomato purée with the fish.*

Some accompaniments to soup

Croutons　*Fry small cubes of bread in hot oil until golden.*

Bacon　*Fry or grill a rasher of bacon until it is crisp; crumble it into
the soup.*

Cheese　*Add a tablespoon of grated cheese.*

Herb bread　*Mix a pinch of dried herbs into some butter and spread
it on bread. Fry, grill or put it in a hot oven to crisp for a few minutes. You can use oil instead of butter.*

Garlic bread　*Prepare as above, using crushed garlic instead of
herbs.*

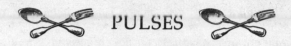

PULSES

Pulses are very good news. They contain plenty of proteins and nutrients and are very much cheaper than meat. Every time you open a tin of baked beans you can enjoy a bonus, because not only is it childishly easy but it is also doing you good, especially if you eat it with toasted wholemeal bread or sprinkle over some grated cheese or top it with an egg. Most people will already be familiar with haricot beans – these are the ones in the baked bean tins – and dried peas, which you may know in the form of mushy peas or pease pudding. You have probably enjoyed lentils in soup. There are lots more. You can buy pulses in two forms, dried or ready cooked in cans. Dried are much cheaper but the snag is that they need to be soaked and cooked, all of which may seem daunting when you are not necessarily sure if you are going to think they are worth the trouble. So I suggest that if you are new to pulses, you first buy them in canned form. Having tried them out you will then know if you think it is worth going to the extra trouble of soaking and cooking the dried variety.

SOAKING DRIED PULSES

You can buy dried pulses loose or in packets. If loose, wash them and pick them over to remove any bits of stone or grit. They can be soaked in one of two ways.

1. Put the pulses into a saucepan, cover in cold water and bring to the boil. Boil for 10 minutes, remove from the heat, cover and leave for an hour. Then proceed to cook them, see next page.
2. Put the pulses into a saucepan, cover in cold water and leave either overnight, or for several hours during the day while you are at college.

Certain pulses, such as soya beans and chickpeas, do need the longer overnight soaking period of at least 12 hours. Red lentils and split peas need no soaking.

COOKING DRIED PULSES

Cook them in the water in which they have soaked, bring to the boil, boil for 10 minutes, cover and simmer. For the appropriate cooking time, see list below. Certain beans such as red kidney beans, soya and butter beans are high in substances which are harmful to the digestion unless they are properly cooked. This means that when you cook them they must be boiled for at least 10 minutes before lowering the heat and allowing them to simmer for the remaining time. To be sure, it is sensible to boil all beans for 10 minutes. Once they have begun to simmer, they will take from 35 minutes to over an hour to cook. When they are tender, drain and add a little salt.

If you add salt while they are cooking, they will never soften.

Approximate cooking times

35 minutes	black eye and flageolet beans, red lentils
40 minutes	butter and pinto beans
50 minutes	chickpeas, red kidney beans
55 minutes	haricot beans
1–1½ hours	soya beans, split peas

Here are some ideas for dealing with some of the different kinds. Although hummus must be made with chickpeas and dhal with lentils, most beans are interchangeable, so it is worth trying some of the dishes even though you may not have the particular variety of bean I have recommended. To estimate quantities reckon on 50 g (2 oz) per serving. It's a good idea to cook at least 225 g (8 oz) since it isn't worth the effort to do less. You can keep the cooked pulses covered in a fridge for several days. If you want to find out more about pulses, read Vegetarian Student *and look out for recipes in Eastern or mid-Eastern cookery books.*

HARICOT BEANS

WITH BACON AND ONION

Heat a frying pan, add a chopped bacon rasher and when the fat begins to run add a chopped onion. Season with a little cinnamon and nutmeg, and cook until the bacon is soft. Drain the cooked beans, add to the pan and heat through. Season with salt and pepper to taste.

WITH TOMATO AND ONION

Heat a tablespoon of oil or cooking fat in a frying pan, add a chopped onion, and cook for about 5 minutes until it is soft. Add a sliced tomato, and cook for 2 or 3 minutes before adding the cooked beans. Season to taste.

WITH TOMATO AND TUNA

Heat a tablespoon of oil, cooking fat or butter in a frying pan, add a sliced tomato and cook for 2 or 3 minutes. Add the contents of a small can of tuna, heat through, breaking it up with a wooden spoon. Then add the cooked beans and a little oregano. Season to taste.

SALAD

Add a squeeze of lemon juice, a tablespoon of oil, some finely chopped onion or garlic to the cold cooked beans. Season to taste. Or proceed as above, then add a very thinly sliced onion, broken into rings and top with the contents of a small tin of tuna.

RED KIDNEY BEANS

WITH TOMATO SAUCE

A good way of using the tomato sauce which is left over from a pasta dish (see page 59). Simply heat the sauce, add a small sliced green or red pepper (seeds removed), a pinch of chilli powder and a teaspoon of Worcester sauce, if you have any. Simmer for about 10 minutes to soften the pepper. Add the cooked beans and heat through.

Red kidney beans are an essential ingredient of chilli con carne; you will find a recipe on page 91.

CHICKPEAS

WITH POTATO, ONION AND SPICES

Heat a tablespoon of oil, margarine or butter in a frying pan, add a chopped onion and 1 potato, peeled and cut into small dice (the smaller the dice, the quicker it will cook). Cook gently until the onion and the potato are soft, about 10 minutes. Add some cinnamon and nutmeg (about ¼ teaspoon of each), stir in the cooked chickpeas. Add a pinch of salt, ½ teaspoon of sugar and heat through.

SALAD

Mix the cold cooked chickpeas with a little finely chopped onion or garlic. Season with a squeeze of lemon juice, a tablespoon of oil and salt and pepper. Add 2 or 3 sliced mushrooms and mix.

Chickpeas also go well with fish. Add some chopped sardines or pilchards or a small tin of tuna. If you like mussels, add the contents of a jar or tin. If you can find the ones in brine, they make an interesting change to those sold in vinegar.

HUMMUS

You may have bought this from a delicatessen and if you like it, might like to make your own. It is basically chickpeas, garlic and tahini – which is sesame seed paste and can be bought in health shops. It needs to be mashed to a purée, so this is another use for the Mouli-légumes (see page 16). You could use a potato masher. Drain and empty a can or mug of cooked chickpeas and mash or put through the Mouli-légumes to make a smooth purée. Using a wooden spoon beat in 2 tablespoons of cooking liquid or liquid from the can, add the juice of a lemon, a finely chopped clove of garlic, 4 tablespoons of tahini and salt to taste.

LENTILS

DHAL

Put 1 mug of red lentils into a saucepan with 2 mugs plus 3 tablespoons of water. Add a bay leaf, a small chopped onion, a crushed clove of garlic, a pinch of ginger and turmeric. Set the pan over a high heat, bring to the boil, lower heat and simmer for about 30 minutes until the lentils are soft and have absorbed the water.

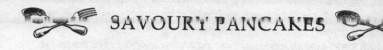

SAVOURY PANCAKES

Pancakes with a savoury filling, topped with grated cheese or a sauce are a delicious way of stretching limited ingredients into a full-sized meal. If you haven't made them before, you might like to try one of the recipes using a pancake or batter mix or even ready-made pancakes. Once you've discovered how delicious they are, try making your own – there's a recipe for pancake batter on page 138.

TO COOK PANCAKES   *(makes 8–12)*

Make the basic batter, adding 1 tablespoon of oil with the liquid. Let it stand for an hour or two.

1. Use a small frying pan, the 18-cm (7-inch) one is ideal.
2. Heat it over a medium heat.
3. Grease the pan with a smear of oil or butter.
4. Pour 2 tablespoons of batter into the pan and tilt it with a circular motion so that the batter runs completely over the base. It should be very thin. If holes appear, dribble in a little batter to cover.
5. Let the pancake cook for 30–60 seconds until the surface is opaque and it is beginning to blister.
6. Use a spatula and your fingers to lift the edge; if the base is golden, turn the pancake over.
7. Cook for about 20 seconds, by which time the other side will be browned. Remove from pan.
8. If not using immediately, stack the pancakes interleaved with strips of greaseproof paper to prevent them sticking together.

Pancakes can be stored for a week in the fridge and they can be frozen. So it's quite practical to make more than you need for one meal. This is also the sort of meal that is good to make when you're cooking for 2 or more people. Pancakes can, of course, also have sweet fillings and there are ideas on page 132.

PANCAKE DISHES

You need to use a shallow ovenproof dish or tin. Allow 2–3 pancakes per person, depending upon appetites. There are ideas for fillings below. The pancakes can be stacked one on top of the other with layers of the filling in between each; or put a tablespoon of filling in the centre of each and roll them up; or, having put the filling in the centre, fold two edges to the middle and the whole thing in half again to form a square – it depends how creative you are feeling.

Once the dish is filled, you can simply top with grated cheese – allow a tablespoon per head – then dab with a little margarine or butter, or sprinkle over a tablespoon or so of oil. Or you can cover them with a tomato sauce (see page 59) or a cheese sauce (see page 139). Allow 300 ml (½ pint) of sauce for 3 to 4 people and finish by sprinkling over a tablespoon or two of grated cheese.

To warm through, either grill: set the dish on the lowest rung and heat through until the top is brown – about 4–5 minutes. Or, heat in the oven at Gas 6/400 °F/200 °C for 10 minutes.

Some suggested fillings

Heat a tablespoon of oil in a frying pan. When it is just beginning to smoke add a chopped onion. Cook for about 5 minutes until it is soft. Add one of the following:

Mushrooms   Allow 50 g (2 oz) per person, slice and cook over a moderate heat for 3 or 4 minutes. Stir in a teaspoon of flour, 4 tablespoons of yogurt or top of the milk and heat to boiling point. Remove from the heat and season with salt, pepper, and a pinch of dried mixed herbs or thyme. If you have a piece of ham, you can lay this on the pancake before topping with the filling.

Spinach   When the onion is soft, add 1 sliced mushroom per person. Let it cook for 3 or 4 minutes, then add a pinch of nutmeg. You can use fresh spinach, in which case allow 100 g (4 oz) per person and cook it as on page 114, or use a small packet of frozen or a can of spinach. Heat it and drain it thoroughly. Add to the mixture.

Chicken livers   When the onion is soft, add 1 sliced mushroom per person. Let it cook for 3 or 4 minutes then add a pinch of nutmeg. Chop 50 g (2 oz) chicken livers per person, discarding the green pieces which are bitter. Add to the pan and cook for 2 or 3 minutes to brown them. Mix with 2 or 3 tablespoons of yogurt and season with salt, pepper and herbs.

Mince   Prepare as for chicken livers, using mince instead. You can stir in a tablespoon of tomato purée instead of yogurt.

Chicken   Prepare as for chicken livers using 2 or 3 tablespoons of cooked chicken per person.

Fish   Prepare as for chicken livers using 2 or 3 tablespoons of cooked or tinned fish per person. Try tuna or salmon.

Cabbage and chicken   When the onion is soft, add some finely sliced cabbage. Cook for several minutes and flavour it with a few drops of soy sauce and some pepper; or add a teaspoonful of sugar and one of vinegar. Stir in 1 or 2 tablespoons of chopped cooked chicken per person. Moisten with yogurt.

Bacon, onion and tomato   Add a chopped rasher of bacon per person to 1 or 2 chopped onions and fry for 5 minutes. Stir in a small can of Italian tomatoes, add some pepper and a pinch of oregano, basil or marjoram.

Bacon, leeks and tomato   Prepare as previous filling, but use leeks instead of onion. See page 115 for how to prepare leeks. Cut them into thin rings.

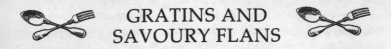

GRATINS AND SAVOURY FLANS

A 'gratin' is a term used to describe a dish which after being cooked in the oven or under the grill is covered by a golden-brown crust. This browning process is often aided by the addition of a sprinkling of grated cheese and breadcrumbs (see page 145 for how to make dried breadcrumbs). All sorts of things can be prepared in this manner: vegetables, fish, meat and pulses. Sometimes the food is mixed with egg and milk which forms a custard, or it is covered with a sauce. Many ideas for gratins are similar to those used for filling savoury flans, such as quiches.

You probably won't feel that it is worth making these sort of dishes when you are cooking only for yourself, but they make very pleasant, cheap meals when cooked for two or more. Most of them – with the exception of the pastry-based flans – can be cooked on top of the stove and then browned under a hot grill. Pastry-based flans must be cooked in the oven. The quantities given are sufficient for 2 or 3 helpings unless otherwise stated.

CAULIFLOWER CHEESE

Divide a cauliflower into florets. Put 1 cm (½ inch) of water into a saucepan, bring to the boil, add salt, add cauliflower, cover, and cook until it is tender – about 5–10 minutes. Drain it. Make a cheese sauce (see page 139) and add a teaspoon of made mustard. Put the cauliflower in a dish, pour over the sauce, top with 2 or 3 tablespoons of grated cheese. Brown for 5–10 minutes in a hot oven at Gas 7/425°F/22°C or under a hot grill.

TOMATOES

Allow 1 large tomato per person. Cut them in half, cut a cross in each cut face, and push in very thin slivers of garlic – how much depends on how much you like garlic. Add salt and pepper and top with dried breadcrumbs. Put under a hot grill for 5 minutes or so to cook and brown the top, or in a hot oven Gas 7/425 °F/220 °C.

LEEKS

Wash and prepare 2 or 3 leeks and cook them as on page 115. Put them in a shallow heatproof dish and either sprinkle with grated cheese and dot with a little margarine or butter, or cover with a cheese sauce (see page 139). Sprinkle with a tablespoon of cheese and put under a hot grill to brown for about 5 minutes.

POTATO

Grease an ovenproof dish. Peel and slice 450 g (1 lb) of potatoes thinly. Lay them in the dish, adding salt, pepper, 1 tablespoon of cheese and a few little dabs of butter the size of a pea on each layer. Add enough milk almost to cover them. Cook at Gas 6/400°F/200°C for 45 minutes until the top is brown and the milk is absorbed.

If you like, use stock instead of milk and add an onion cut in thin slices.

POTATO, ONION, TOMATO AND ANCHOVY

Slice an onion thinly and cook it in a little oil until it is soft (about 5 minutes). Mix with the contents of a medium can of Italian tomatoes. Peel 450–700 g (1–1½ lb) potatoes and slice thinly. Open a can of anchovies. In a greased ovenproof dish place layers of potato, tomato and onion, and anchovy, making the last layer tomato and onion. Sprinkle over the top a little oregano or basil and some thyme. Top with a couple of tablespoons of grated cheese or breadcrumbs, and pour over the oil from the anchovy can. Cook for 40 minutes at Gas 6/400°F/200°C.

You could cook both the above potato gratins very gently in a saucepan on top of the stove before emptying them into a shallow dish, topping with the cheese or breadcrumbs and browning under a grill.

COURGETTE AND TOMATO

Slice 450 g (1 lb) courgettes into rings about 1 cm (½ inch) thick. Sprinkle with salt and leave for 30 minutes to drain. Pat dry with kitchen paper. Heat 2 tablespoons of oil in a frying pan and cook the *courgettes until they are soft, turning the pieces from time to time (about 10 minutes). Put in a shallow heatproof dish. Cut 450 g (1 lb) tomatoes into quarters and cook until soft in a little oil, or use the contents of a medium can of Italian tomatoes. Season with salt, pepper and a pinch of basil, oregano or thyme. Put in the dish with the courgettes. Top with 2 or 3 tablespoons grated cheese or dried breadcrumbs, mixed, if you like, with a finely chopped clove of garlic. Sprinkle over a teaspoon of oil or dot with butter. Place in the oven at Gas 5/375 °F/190 °C for 10–15 minutes or brown under a moderate grill until it is heated through.*

Use the above recipes for all sorts of other vegetables, such as mushrooms (allow 75–100 g (3–4 oz) per head), leeks or aubergines or use a can of sweetcorn, haricot or butter beans or your own cooked pulses (see page 71).

MINCE AND LENTILS   *(4 servings)*

    1 mug red lentils
    2 mugs water
    basic mince recipe using 175 g (6 oz) mince (see page 91)
    4 tablespoons dried breadcrumbs

Put the lentils into a saucepan, cover them with water and bring to the boil. Lower the heat and let them simmer for 20 minutes. Meanwhile prepare the mince recipe. Mix the lentils with the meat sauce and place in a shallow heatproof dish. Top with breadcrumbs. Heat the grill for 5 minutes, then place the dish under it for 4 or 5 minutes to brown the crumbs.

FISH AND MUSHROOM GRATIN   *(2 servings)*

    225 g (8 oz) white fish fillet, such as cod, haddock, coley,
        plaice or 2 fish steaks
    50 g (2 oz) mushrooms, sliced
    1 onion, chopped
    2 eggs
    ½ mug creamy milk
    salt and pepper
    1 teaspoon parsley or mixed herbs
    1 tablespoon grated cheese or breadcrumbs

Grease an ovenproof dish with oil. Place the fish in the dish, top with the mushrooms and the onion. Beat the eggs with the milk, add a pinch of salt and some pepper and the herbs, and pour over the fish. Top with the cheese or breadcrumbs and cook at Gas 3/325 °F/160 °C for 30–40 minutes. Instead of the egg and milk custard mixture you could use a white or cheese sauce (see page 138) or a can of Italian tomatoes, including their juice.

QUICHES

The name 'quiche' is used in current English to describe any kind of savoury flan with a custard base. Many of the fillings could be used simply as the basis for a gratin, so if making pastry is something you'd rather not do, you will still find some ideas for dishes to make from the list below. Pastry recipes are on page 140. If you are pressed for time you could buy a pastry mix or ready-made pastry, either fresh or frozen. Directions for use will be on the packets.

BASIC QUICHE   *(2 servings)*

> 2 eggs
> 6 tablespoons milk, curd cheese or plain yogurt
> salt and pepper
> pinch of nutmeg (optional)
> filling (see next page)
> pastry to line an 18-cm (7-inch) flan ring or tin

Beat the eggs with the milk and cheese or yogurt, add a pinch of salt, some pepper and the nutmeg, if using, and stir in your chosen filling. Pour into a pastry base and sprinkle over a tablespoon of grated cheese, or put dabs of butter the size of a pea over the top, (use about a tablespoon). Cook at Gas 5/375 °F/190 °C for 30–35 minutes. Test by putting a knife point into the centre. If it comes out clean, the quiche is done. If not, leave it a few minutes longer.

When the quiche comes from the oven it will be puffed and risen. As it cools, the filling settles and even if you reheat it, it won't rise again. You can eat quiche hot, warm or cold.

Suggested fillings to be added to basic quiche

Bacon   *Cut 3 or 4 rashers into small pieces and fry them until crisp without adding any extra fat or oil to the pan.*

Cheese   *Grate 50–75 g (2–3 oz) of cheese – almost any kind will do – and stir half into the mixture. Sprinkle the rest over the surface.*

Bacon with onion   *Chop 2 rashers and an onion. Fry the bacon until the fat runs, then add the onion. Cook for 5–10 minutes until the onion is soft and the bacon crisp.*

Onion   *Chop or slice 2 onions, cook gently in butter until very soft, 10–15 minutes.*

Spinach   *Wash 75–100 g (3–4 oz) spinach in several changes of water, as it contains a lot of grit. Cook it until soft in a little salted water, drain well and chop. While it is cooking, fry a small chopped onion in a little oil or butter. Mix the spinach and onion together before stirring into the quiche mixture. If you like, use a packet of frozen spinach.*

Mushrooms   *Chop some mushrooms – 75–100 g (3–4 oz) – and cook them with a little chopped onion in some oil or butter for 5 minutes.*

Broccoli   *Prepare as for spinach. Wash under tap – broccoli doesn't contain as much grit as spinach.*

Leek and bacon   *Use 2 leeks cut into rings, and prepare as for bacon with onion.*

Chicken livers   *Use 50–75 g (2–3 oz) of livers (or use the liver from a packet of giblets inside a roasting chicken). Cut into 2 or 3 pieces, discarding any green bits, they are bitter. Cook the pieces in a little butter with a chopped onion.*

Tomato   *Slice 2 or 3 tomatoes, sprinkle them with salt and leave for 30 minutes. This will make some of their liquid run out. Dry them with a piece of kitchen paper, lay on the pastry base, add a sprinkling of basil or oregano then pour the quiche mixture over.*

Tuna   *Prepare a tomato as above, and lay on the pastry base. Drain a can of tuna, break up the fish with a fork and add to the quiche mixture.*

Sweetcorn, ratatouille, asparagus   *For very quick quiches, buy these in cans and use as fillings. Canned asparagus can be bought more cheaply in pieces – worth looking out for on supermarket shelves.*

Onion, ham and potato   *Heat a tablespoon of oil in a frying pan. When it is just beginning to smoke, add a chopped onion. Cook until the onion is soft (about 5 minutes). Add a slice of ham, cut into small pieces, and a couple of potatoes (if they are already cooked, cut them into slices; if they are raw, grate them).*

Onion, frankfurter and potato   *Make as above, substituting a sliced frankfurter for the ham.*

Ham and leeks   *Slice 2 leeks into rings. Cook gently in a little butter or margarine until soft (about 10 minutes). Add a slice of ham, cut into small pieces.*

Ham and banana   *Cut a slice of ham into small pieces and stir into the quiche mixture, together with a sliced banana.*

Chicken and mushroom   *Heat a tablespoon of oil or butter. When it is hot, add 3 or 4 sliced mushrooms and a chopped onion. Cook for about 5 minutes, then stir in ½ mug of cooked chicken, cut into small pieces.*

Instead of being mixed with the egg and milk custard, many of the above fillings could be topped by a white or cheese sauce (see page 138). If you don't want to make your own sauce, you could use a sauce mix. Simply pour the hot sauce over the other ingredients in the pastry base – 150 ml (½ pint) will be sufficient – top with grated cheese or dried breadcrumbs and cook as above.

If you decide to omit the pastry and prefer to make a gratin, you can simply brown the whole dish in the oven at Gas 5/375 °F/190 °C for 15–20 minutes or under a hot grill until it is heated through.

BAKING FOOD IN PARCELS

When you are pressed for time or cooking for several people, a wonderfully easy way of preparing food is to wrap it in greaseproof paper or foil, make it into parcels and bake it in the oven. In 20 to 30 minutes it is done, all the flavours and juices are contained and there are no pans to wash. You simply put a parcel on each plate, everyone opens their own and discards the wrappings. Whether you use paper or foil will probably be decided by economy. Foil is perhaps slightly easier to use but it is more expensive (you can use it more than once if you rinse it after use in hot water, the foil loses its lustre but not its cooking use). It's worth doing parcels when you are using the oven for other things. You might bake jacket potatoes and have a fruit crumble for pudding.

TO MAKE THE PARCELS

Use either greaseproof paper or aluminium foil; if you haven't got either you could use a pice of thin white paper. You need an oblong large enough to amply enclose each portion of food, leaving room for air to circulate. Fold in half and if you are using paper, cut it into the shape of a semicircle (it will be easier to crimp the finished edges); foil need not be cut. Open out flat and grease – with oil or fat. Lay the food on one half, bring the other half right over and fold the edges down twice to form a hem, crimp the edges to form pleats and seal the parcel. Foil will cling to itself, paper may be a little more difficult, if necessary put in a few staples or a couple of pins. With practice, it gets easier. Put the parcels on a baking sheet and cook them in the centre of the oven at Gas 5/375°F/190°C. If you are using meat that has been frozen, don't forget to make sure it has completely defrosted before it is cooked.

CHICKEN, RABBIT OR TURKEY JOINT

Sprinkle each joint with lemon juice, a pinch of salt and pepper, ¼ teaspoon of thyme or mixed herbs, a teaspoon of oil or a dab of margarine or butter. You could add a sliced mushroom, or a tablespoon of grated cheese; or spread with mustard and a teaspoon of honey. Cook for 25 minutes.

LAMB CHOP

Put a little chopped onion and a sliced tomato with thyme and a pinch of salt and pepper on top of the chop. Or instead of onion and tomato, use mushrooms and a slice of cheese. Cook for 25 minutes.

PORK CHOP

Sprinkle the chop with lemon juice, a little sage or rosemary, a pinch of salt and pepper and add a thin slice of butter. Or add some sliced apple, a sprinkling of sugar, a small dab of mustard and salt and pepper. Cook for 35 minutes.

GAMMON STEAK

Put a smear of mustard and a teaspoon of sugar on the steak. Add some pieces of orange and season with salt and pepper. Or add a little chopped onion, some sliced apple, a teaspoon of honey, a sprinkling of lemon juice and salt and pepper. Cook for 25 minutes.

MACKEREL OR HERRING

Spread the fish with mustard, sprinkle on some lemon juice, salt, pepper and a little parsley. Then add a little butter. Cook for 20 minutes.

FISH STEAK

Use cod, coley or haddock. Sprinkle the fish with lemon juice, add a sliced tomato or mushrooms, salt, pepper and parsley or mixed herbs. Cook for 20 minutes.

VEGETABLES

You can bake vegetables in foil. Butter the foil well, slice the vegetables, add salt and pepper, fold up the parcel and put on a baking dish. Carrots and courgettes will take 35–40 minutes, onions and parsnips 45–50 minutes.

FRUIT

Sprinkle a sliced apple or banana with a little lemon juice and perhaps a pinch of cinnamon or nutmeg. Add some sugar, honey or marmalade. Cook for 15 minutes.

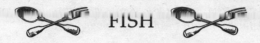 FISH

It isn't always easy to find a fishmonger, and you may have to limit your fish-buying to the frozen variety; however, fish that is frozen retains its natural goodness and will provide you with a meal that is relatively cheap and quick and easy to prepare. Fresh fish should be eaten the day it is bought or kept for no longer than 24 hours in a fridge. To be certain it is fresh make sure it does not have a strong smell, that the flesh is firm, the gills red and the eyes bright. A fishmonger will clean and gut such fish as herring and mackerel for you, and if you ask him he will probably remove the centre bones too. Frozen whole fish should be thawed before cooking – times are usually on the package, but allow a couple of hours in the kitchen. You can cook fish steaks and fillets from frozen, again read the instructions on the packet.

Fish can be cooked in a variety of ways, all of them simple and quite quick. For one person allow 175–225 g (6–8 oz) of fish fillet or 225–275 g (8–10 oz) of fish on the bone or whole fish.

GRILLED FISH

Heat the grill for 5 minutes until it is very hot. Remove the grid from the grill pan, add 2 tablespoons of oil, margarine or butter and perhaps ½ teaspoon of herbs such as thyme, fennel or dill. Put the pan under the grill to melt the fat. When it is sizzling add the fish steak or fillet, spoon some fat over it, and season with salt, pepper and perhaps a little lemon juice. Put the pan under the heat and cook until the flesh is firm and opaque, about 5–10 minutes. There is no need to turn it but keep your eye on it, so it doesn't burn.

If you are cooking a whole fish, first cut two diagonal slits in each side, and season it with salt and pepper. Cook as above but give it 2 minutes on one side and then turn it over and cook for about 8 minutes. The fish is done when the eyes become white and opaque.

POACHED FISH

Put a mug of milk or milk and water in a pan and bring it to the boil. Lower the heat and add the fish. Cover, and let it simmer very gently for 5–10 minutes, until the flesh is firm and white.

FRIED FISH

Heat 2 tablespoons of oil or cooking fat in a frying pan. When it just begins to smoke, add the fish. Fry over a medium heat until golden, turn the fish, lower the heat and let it cook for another 5–6 minutes until the flesh is firm and opaque.

Coatings for fried fish

To prevent fish that is fried from sticking to the pan and also to give it a crisp coat, it can be prepared in one of several ways:
Flour   *Put 2 tablespoons of flour on a plate, add a pinch of salt and pepper, roll the fish in this to cover all sides.*
Flour and milk   *Dip the fish in flour as above, then in a little milk and then in more flour.*
Flour, egg and breadcrumbs   *Dip the fish in flour as above, followed by beaten egg and then in 2 tablespoons of dried breadcrumbs. These can be bought or homemade (see page 145).*

BAKED FISH

See the chapter on baking food in parcels, pages 84–5.

FISH AND CHIPS

To cook authentic fish and chips you need a deep-frying basket and lots of oil to give the batter and potatoes their crisp outer texture and soft interior. It's expensive and can be messy and smelly. If you want to eat chips with home-cooked fish, the most practical solution would probably be to buy frozen oven chips. They simply require heating – see the instructions on the packets.

FISH CAKES

$\frac{1}{2}$ mug cooked fish
$\frac{1}{2}$ mug mashed potato
1 teaspoon finely chopped onion
few drops lemon juice

salt and pepper
beaten egg or milk
1 tablespoon oil or cooking fat

Mix all the ingredients together except the fat, adding a pinch of salt and some pepper, and egg or milk to bind them. Dampen your hands, to prevent the mixture sticking, and form it into two flat cakes. Heat the oil or fat in a frying pan over a medium heat. When it is hot, add the fish cakes. Cook briskly, turning once, until both sides are golden, 5–10 minutes.

Fish cakes can also be coated in flour or flour, egg and breadcrumbs, see above.

KIPPERS

Put kippers in a jug, fill up with boiling water. Leave for 5 minutes. Drain. Eat with a lump of margarine or butter.

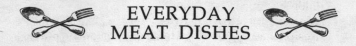

EVERYDAY MEAT DISHES

You may feel that meat is an expensive luxury which you have got to learn to live without. On the other hand, the idea of living without meat may appal you. It is quite possible to maintain a healthy diet with no meat at all, but if you feel you can afford it and you like it, meat does provide a lot of protein. If you have a good canteen which provides you with a lunch containing meat, then you needn't worry about cooking any in the evenings for yourself. Fortunately cheaper cuts of meat contain just as much protein as the more expensive ones. However, it is worth remembering that some of the cheaper cuts also have a high proportion of fat. They are therefore not necessarily always a good buy as you will find that once you have cut away the fat, the actual edible portion that remains may have become relatively costly.

In this and the two following chapters you will find ideas for meals for 1 person and others which are more suitable when cooking for a group. There are notes on page 31 about buying and storing meat.

MINCE

Because mince does not keep very well, you should cook it on the day you buy it, or keep it for not more than 24 hours in a fridge. It is worth avoiding the cheaper brands of mince which do contain a disproportionate amount of fat. Fresh mince should look pink and not brown or grey. Beef is the most readily obtainable but sometimes you will be able to buy minced lamb or pork. I suggest that you cook 225 g (8 oz) at a time because even if it is only for one, you can use it to make two meals. When reheating, remember to make sure you bring it to boiling point to kill any bacteria that may have formed.

BASIC MINCE RECIPE   *(2 servings)*

> 225 g (8 oz) mince
> 1 onion, chopped
> Half a medium can of Italian tomatoes or 225 g (8 oz)
>   fresh tomatoes, sliced *or* 2 teaspoons of tomato purée
>   and ½ mug of stock or water
> salt and pepper
> additional flavouring (see below)

Heat a frying pan over a medium heat. When it is hot add the mince. Cook until it is brown all over, stirring all the time. Add the chopped onion and mix well, then cook for 3 or 4 minutes. Add a pinch of salt and some pepper and additional flavouring. Bring to the boil, cover, lower the heat and simmer for 15–20 minutes.

Suggested flavourings

A green pepper, chopped and deseeded
Small can of baked beans
Sliced courgettes or aubergine
Clove of garlic, chopped
A tablespoon of dried fruit or nuts
Quarter of a tablespoon of dried herbs, such as mixed, thyme, oregano
Half a teaspoon of curry powder
A carrot, chopped small – add at the same time as the onion
75 or 100 g (3 or 4 oz) mushrooms, sliced
A few drops of Worcester sauce or mushroom ketchup

You can use one of these ideas or a selection; it is worth experimenting. The only rule is not to confuse the whole thing by having too many different flavours.

CHILLI CON CARNE   *(4 servings)*

This is made exactly as the basic recipe. When the mince and onion have browned, add 1 or 2 teaspoons dried chilli powder. (Make sure you use chilli powder and not the very hot pepper which is made of chillies.) Let the chilli powder cook a minute or two, add a tablespoon of tomato purée, a medium can of Italian tomatoes and a can of red kidney beans. (Or you can use dried kidney beans, see the chapter on pulses, page 71. Remember that soaked kidney beans must be boiled for 10 minutes in order to kill any toxic substance.) Bring to the boil, then cover, lower the heat and cook the chilli con carne for 50–60 minutes.

This is even nicer if made the day ahead, cooled, kept in the fridge overnight and reheated. It needs to be brought quickly to boiling point and then simmered for 15–20 minutes.

STUFFED VEGETABLES

Cook basic mince recipe with flavourings of your choice to stuff vegetables such as tomatoes, peppers, courgettes or marrow, aubergine, mushroom and cabbage. Make sure you season the mixture well. The quantity of mince is enough for 2 or 3 servings. To make it more filling, you could add a couple of tablespoons of cooked rice or fresh breadcrumbs (see page 145).

The stuffed vegetables can be cooked in a shallow dish or tin in the oven with the addition of a little water. Or make a simple tomato sauce. Heat the contents of a medium can of Italian tomatoes in a small pan, flavour it with a teaspoon of sugar, some finely chopped onion, a pinch of salt and some pepper, and ½ teaspoon of oregano or basil. When it is hot, pour around the vegetables in the dish.

Tomatoes   *Allow 1 or 2 per person, cut in half. Scoop out the flesh with a teaspoon and mix this with the basic mince. Season well. Fill the halves and cook at Gas 5/375 °F/190 °C for 10–15 minutes, or put under a hot grill for 5 minutes.*

Green peppers   *Allow 1 per person. Cut off the stalk end and discard the seeds, which are hot. Cook the peppers for 5 minutes in boiling salted water. Drain and fill with the basic mince. Cook at Gas 5/375 °F/190 °C for 30 minutes.*

Courgettes and aubergines   *Allow 1 medium one per person. Cut in half lengthways, sprinkle with salt and leave to drain for 30 minutes. Wipe with kitchen paper. Scoop out the centre and mix with the basic mince. Fill and cook for 30–40 minutes at Gas 5/375 °F/190 °C.*

Marrow   *Choose a marrow about 30 cm (12 inches) long. This will serve 3–4 people. Cook it for 3 minutes in a saucepan of boiling salted water. Cut it in half lengthways, scoop out and discard the seeds, using a spoon. Fill with the basic mince. As marrow is fairly tasteless, it's important the filling should be well seasoned. Put the halves together and either tie with string or skewer them together. Cook at*

Gas 5/375 °F/190 °C for about an hour, until the marrow is soft when pricked with a pointed knife. Cook a little longer if it is still hard.

Mushrooms   Allow 1 or 2 very large flat mushrooms per person. Cut off stalks, chop them and add to the basic mince. Grill the mushrooms gently for a few minutes, top with the filling and put under a high heat for a few minutes, until heated throughout.

Cabbage   Allow 2 large leaves per person. Cook them in boiling salted water for 3 or 4 minutes to soften them. Drain well, pat dry with kitchen paper and cut away any hard stalk. Put a tablespoon of the basic mince in each leaf and roll up. Cook them in tomato sauce (see above) at Gas 4/350 °F/180 °C in a covered dish or casserole for 45 minutes.

COTTAGE PIE

Make the basic mince recipe, flavouring it with ½ medium can of Italian tomatoes and a dash of Worcester sauce. Put into a heatproof dish and top with mashed potatoes – use about 450 g (1 lb) (see page 52). If the sauce and the potatoes are hot, set the dish under a hot grill for 4 or 5 minutes. If using cold potato, put in the oven at Gas 7/425 °F/220 °C for about 20 minutes to heat through and brown.

If you wish, dot the top with little pieces of butter or margarine, or sprinkle with grated cheese or a little nutmeg or paprika.

PITTA BREAD FILLED WITH MINCE

This is a good party standby. Hardly any washing up and your guests can fill the bread themselves. Allow 1 pitta cut in half crossways and 100 g (4 oz) mince per person. Make the basic mince recipe, add 2 tablespoons of dried fruit, such as sultanas or raisins, season well with a teaspoon of cinnamon and one of thyme, 2 tablespoons of salted peanuts, and pepper. Taste, you may not need any additional salt. Warm the bread in a moderate oven – Gas 4/350 °F/180 °C – for 5 minutes. Set the mince mixture in a bowl on the table. Let everyone help themselves.

MOUSSAKA   (4 servings)

This dish originates from Greece. Traditionally it is made up of a meat sauce, usually lamb, topped with aubergines and a cheese sauce.

The sauce is thickened by adding egg yolks (see page 146 for how to separate eggs). In place of aubergines, you could use courgettes or even potatoes. It would make a very good dish for a party.

450 g (1 lb) aubergines, courgettes or cooked potato
2 tablespoons oil
1 onion, chopped
1 clove of garlic, chopped (optional)
350 g (12 oz) minced lamb or beef
1 teaspoon plain flour
medium can Italian tomatoes
salt and pepper
½ teaspoon oregano
cheese sauce (see page 139)
2 eggs yolks (optional)
1 tablespoon grated cheese

If using aubergines or courgettes, slice them in rings about 1 cm (½ inch) thick, sprinkle with salt and leave for 30 minutes in a colander to draw out the moisture. Wipe them with a piece of kitchen paper. Heat the oil in a frying pan or saucepan and when it just begins to smoke, add the aubergine or courgette slices. Cook them for a few minutes over a medium heat until they are soft, then remove. If using potatoes, cook them in their skins (see page 49). Slice them without peeling.

Add the chopped onion to the pan – adding a little more oil if necessary – cook until it is soft and beginning to brown, then add the chopped garlic, if using. After 2 or 3 minutes, stir in the mince and cook over a medium heat, stirring from time to time until it is brown. Add the flour, mix, and pour over the tomatoes and their juice. Season with a pinch of salt, some pepper and the oregano. Bring to the boil, cover and lower the heat.

Make the cheese sauce. When it thickens, remove from the heat, add the egg yolks, if using, and mix. The yolks will thicken and enrich the sauce – it's important to take the pan from the heat as otherwise the yolks may curdle and you will have a sauce that looks like scrambled eggs.

Assemble the moussaka in an ovenproof dish: the meat sauce, then the sliced aubergines, courgettes or potatoes, then the cheese sauce. Sprinkle with grated cheese. Cook at Gas 5/375 °F/190 °C for 40–45 minutes until the top is golden.

MEAT LOAF (4 servings)

350 g (12 oz) mince
1 onion, chopped very finely
4 tablespoons fresh breadcrumbs (see page 145)
1 egg, beaten
4 tablespoons water or stock
1 teaspoon tomato purée
few drops Worcester sauce
salt and pepper
½ teaspoon herbs, such as mixed, thyme, parsley

Grease a loaf tin with a little oil. Mix all the ingredients together, using a pinch of salt and some pepper, and put them in the tin. Bake at Gas 4/350 °F/180 °C for 45 minutes. If you haven't got a loaf tin, form the mixture into a loaf shape and enclose it in foil.

Variations

Use rolled oats instead of breadcrumbs; put 2 or 3 rashers of bacon across the top before you bake the loaf; mix 2 or 3 sliced mushrooms into the mixture; add 1 teaspoon soy sauce instead of the Worcester sauce, and go easy on the salt.
Sausagemeat loaf   *As above, but substitute sausagemeat for the mince, or make it with half and half.*

MEAT BALLS (2 servings)

Mix 175 g (6 oz) mince with a finely chopped onion, 2 tablespoons fresh breadcrumbs, a pinch of salt and some pepper, a teaspoon of tomato purée and a beaten egg. Add the egg gradually – don't make the mixture too wet. Dampen your hands to stop the mixture sticking and form it into six meat balls. Either grill under a hot grill for about 8 minutes turning them once, or fry them in a little oil.

If you like, add a tablespoon of grated cheese to the mixture; or a teaspoon of mint and one of cumin; or use rolled oats instead of breadcrumbs.

HAMBURGERS

For two hamburgers allow 100 g (4 oz) mince. Mix with a teaspoon of finely chopped onion, and a pinch of salt and some pepper. Shape into two flat cakes about 1 cm (½ inch) thick. Heat a little oil or cooking fat in a frying pan. Cook over a high heat allowing about 5 minutes each side, or grill, making sure the grill is very hot before you begin. If you cook hamburgers and meat balls with fierce heat, they will not break up and will be hot right through.

Variations

Add a tablespoon of fresh breadcrumbs or grated cheese to the mixture; or a pinch of dry mustard; or top with grated plain or blue-vein cheese, sweetcorn and chopped apple, chilli sauce or pickles.

Potato burger   Use equal quantities of mince and mashed potato.
Sausage burger   Use sausagemeat instead of mince.

SAUSAGES

To cook sausages, either grill or fry them. They will take about 10–15 minutes and don't need any additional oil or fat. Cook them under or over a moderate heat, turning them occasionally so that they cook evenly. As a general rule the more expensive the sausages, the more meat content.

Smoked sausages such as frankfurters can be eaten cold just as they are, or if to be eaten hot they are normally cooked in water. See instructions on the packet. If buying loose, put them in a pan of boiling water and let them just simmer for 10–15 minutes. If they boil, they will split and burst.

LIVER AND KIDNEYS

Both liver and kidneys can be cooked very quickly and simply, and both are good and cheap sources of nourishment. Ox and pig's liver are cheaper than those of lamb or calf. To tenderize the cheaper types and prevent them tasting too strong, it is a good idea to soak them for about half an hour in some milk (maybe there is a friendly cat around who will enjoy drinking the milk when you have done with it). If the liver is cooked very quickly, it is tender and pleasant to eat so there is no need to braise it for hours – the result of cooking it this way is often very disappointing.

FRIED LIVER AND ONIONS

This is the simplest and quickest way of cooking liver.

> 1 tablespoon oil or cooking fat
> 1 onion, chopped
> 1 teaspoon sugar
> 100 g (4 oz) ox or pig's liver
> salt and pepper
> ¼ teaspoon mixed herbs
> 1 tablespoon water, or orange juice, or tomato juice,
>   or wine

Heat the oil or fat and when it is hot add the chopped onion and sugar (the sugar will help to brown the onion). Cook until it is brown, 5–10 minutes. Cut the liver into very thin strips – you'll need a sharp knife. Add to the pan and cook very briskly, turning the meat over, for 2–3 minutes. Add a pinch of salt, some pepper, herbs and the liquid. As soon as it is bubbling, serve.

You could stir in a teaspoon of made mustard, add a few chopped mushrooms or a chopped tomato and finish it off by adding a tablespoon of plain yogurt.

KIDNEYS WITH MUSTARD

Use lamb's kidneys, ox or pig's need a longer cooking time and are more suitable for such dishes as steak and kidney.

> 2 lamb's kidneys
> 1 tablespoon oil or cooking fat
> 1 teaspoon made mustard
> salt and pepper
> 1 tablespoon plain yogurt or top of the milk

The kidneys must have the outer fat and membrane removed. The butcher will do this for you, but if you buy them pre-packed you might find there is still a thin skin surrounding the kidneys. It will come away quite easily if you first slit it with a pointed knife. Cut the kidneys in half lengthways and cut out the small core of fat inside – scissors are quite a help here. Cut each half into two or three slices.

Heat the oil or fat in a frying pan and when it is foaming add the kidneys. Cook them gently for 5–10 minutes, stirring from time to time. Add the mustard, a pinch of salt and some pepper. Stir in the yogurt or milk and serve.

If you have any Worcester sauce, a few drops of this is a pleasant addition. You could make this a more substantial dish by frying a chopped onion before adding the kidneys. Put the onion to one side of the pan while the kidneys are cooking. A few sliced mushrooms or a sliced tomato can be added when the kidneys are cooked – stir over a high heat for 2 or 3 minutes before adding seasoning.

CASSEROLES

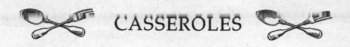

Casseroles are well worth making when cooking for several people, especially as you can cook vegetables in the same pot. They make a wonderful, warming meal for a group on a cold winter's day.

The long, slow cooking of a casserole in the oven or in a pan on top of the stove was devised for the cheaper cuts of meat. You'll find an enormous number of recipes for this type of meal in other cookery books, and they have their origins in many different countries, which adds to the fun. Rather than list a lot of alternative recipes, I think you might find it more useful if I outline the basic technique for cooking a casserole or a stew, with some ideas for variations. Having tried it a few times, you can enjoy making new discoveries from other sources.

If you are going to cook a casserole in the oven, you will need an ovenproof pot. If it is also flameproof, so that you can use it for the preliminary top-of-the-stove cooking as well, so much the better. (See the notes on equipment on page 17.) If your pot is not flameproof, you will have to use a frying pan to begin with. When planning to cook the whole thing on the top of the stove, use a large, heavy pan if possible. It is important that the stew simmers, which means that it cooks just below boiling point: the surface will move a little, and an occasional bubble will rise. If the stew is allowed to boil for a long time, the meat will be tough.

BASIC CASSEROLE METHOD

1. Heat the casserole/frying pan/saucepan over a medium heat. When it is hot, add the oil or cooking fat.
2. While the pan is heating, cut the meat into cubes about 3–5 cm (1½–2 inches) square (you can ask the butcher to do this for you). Cut off any gristle and as much fat as possible. Cook chicken or rabbit joints, lamb cutlets, pork rib chops, etc., on the bone.

3. When the oil/fat is hot, add enough meat to barely cover the base of the pan. The idea is to sear and brown each piece, so you may need to do this operation in batches. Cook the pieces of meat over a fairly high heat for 3 or 4 minutes on each side. Remove, and either put them in the dish in which they are to be cooked or keep them warm between two plates. When all the meat is browned, discard all of the fat in the pan.

4. Add 2 tablespoons of fresh oil or cooking fat, and when it is hot lower the heat and add sliced or chopped onion and any other root vegetable. Let them cook and colour for about 5 minutes, stirring once or twice.

5. Sprinkle over the flour, mix well and let the ingredients cook for 2 or 3 minutes, stirring to prevent them from sticking to the pan.

6. Add the liquid, raise the heat and stir until it boils. Add seasonings.

7. Combine meat, vegetables and liquid in the pot in which they are to be cooked. The level of the liquid should be just below the level of the top of the meat; if necessary, add a little more liquid.

8. Cover the pot – if the lid is a bad fit, a piece of aluminium foil under it will help – and either put it in the oven at Gas 3/325 °F/160 °C or place it on the lowest possible heat on top of the stove.

9. Timing will depend on the quality of the meat, but normally a casserole or stew will take a minimum of 1½–2 hours.

Casseroles and stews reheat very successfully, and often the flavour is even better. They should always be left to cool completely, then stored in the fridge. This has an additional advantage, in that the fat will form a layer on the top, which can be removed with a spoon before reheating. When reheating casseroles and stews, it is important that they are brought to boiling point and allowed to simmer for 20 minutes. If reheating in the oven, set it to Gas 4/350 °F/180 °C and let the casserole heat up thoroughly – allow 30–40 minutes. If the pot is earthenware, place it in a cold oven, then adjust the oven setting as indicated above – otherwise the pot will crack as a result of the drastic change of temperature – and allow an extra 10 minutes.

BASIC BEEF CASSEROLE (4 servings)

*Stewing beef includes such cuts as blade, chuck, flank, skirt, leg, shin,
all of which are often sold under the blanket term 'stewing steak'.*

2 tablespoons oil or cooking fat
700 g (1½ lb) stewing steak, cut into cubes
1 onion, sliced or chopped
1 carrot, sliced or chopped
1 tablespoon plain flour
1 mug stock (either water with a stock cube or a tin of beef
   consommé)
½ teaspoon mixed herbs
½ teaspoon salt
pepper

Variations

With tomato   *Add 2 or 3 quartered tomatoes or a medium can of Italian tomatoes before adding the liquid. If using canned tomatoes, their liquid can form part of the liquid in the recipe.*

With mushrooms   *Add 100 g (4 oz) whole mushrooms, either before adding the liquid or about half an hour before the end of cooking time.*

With beans   *Add a can of drained haricot or butter beans half an hour before the end of cooking time.*

With courgettes   *Add 2 or 3 sliced courgettes when adding the onion and carrot.*

With root vegetables   *Add 3 or 4 carrots, turnips, swedes or parsnips, or a mixture of root vegetables when adding the onion.*

With olives   *Add about 50 g (2 oz) black or green olives just before serving.*

With sweetcorn and tomatoes   *Add a medium can of sweetcorn, drained, and 2 or 3 sliced tomatoes, half an hour before the end of cooking time.*

With paprika and yogurt   *Add a chopped clove of garlic and a tablespoon of paprika at the same time as the flour. After cooking for 3 or 4 minutes, stir in a tablespoon of tomato purée. Add the liquid and cook for 1½ hours. Add 4 medium potatoes, peeled and cut in quarters. Cook for 45 minutes. Just before serving, stir in 2 or 3 tablespoons of plain yogurt.*

With red kidney beans and chilli *Stir in 2 teaspoons of chilli powder when adding the flour, cook for 3 or 4 minutes, then stir in a tablespoon of tomato purée. Add the liquid and cook for 1½ hours. Add a drained can of red kidney beans and continue cooking for 30 minutes.*

Bacon or salt pork *Cut 100 g (4 oz) bacon or salt pork into chunks and fry in the hot pan before adding the oil. Taste before adding any salt.*

Tomato purée *Stir a tablespoon of tomato purée into the mixture before adding the liquid.*

Red wine or beer *Add ½ mug of red wine or beer as part of the liquid.*

Garlic *Add a crushed or finely chopped clove of garlic after the onion has softened.*

The last four ideas could be combined with other variations to add flavour and interest.

BASIC LAMB CASSEROLE

Stewing lamb comes from the breast, scrag end and middle neck and therefore has a high proportion of bone and is rather fatty. The fillet end of the leg can be used, in which case cut the meat from the bone (or ask the butcher to do this), then cut into cubes, as for beef. For meat on the bone allow 225 g (8 oz) per person. Cut away as much fat as possible.

You can make a basic lamb stew using similar ingredients as for beef; lamb goes especially well with mushrooms, sliced courgettes, haricot or butter beans, paprika and garlic. The herbs to use are thyme, rosemary, oregano. Tomatoes seem to enhance the flavour of lamb particularly.

BASIC CHICKEN, TURKEY OR RABBIT CASSEROLE

You can casserole chicken, turkey or rabbit pieces. Follow the basic method given on page 99. A chicken casserole will be ready in 45 minutes; rabbit and turkey will take longer – 1–1½ hours. Add different flavours to these casseroles: mushrooms, courgettes, sliced green peppers, a few whole green or black olives, tomatoes or tomato purée. You can also flavour them with red or white wine. Rabbit will be enhanced if you add a tablespoon of marmalade or redcurrant jelly to the pot. Herbs to use might be thyme, savory, tarragon or parsley.

CURRIES

Indian restaurants provide a fairly inexpensive way of eating out, and if you like this type of food you may well want to try making a curry yourself. The basic technique for many Indian dishes is similar to that of stewing and casseroling. It is worth getting a book which deals specifically with this type of cooking, and having decided to make a curry it is worth investing in the different spices. Bought curry powder just doesn't seem to give a true flavour. Many of the spices used can be added to other types of cooking, so you won't be wasting your money. To encourage you to try, here is a very simple curry. It is made with chicken pieces but you could use cubed lamb, pork or beef, allowing 100–175 g (4–6 oz) meat per person.

A BASIC CURRY POWDER

Mix together the following: 2 teaspoons each of coriander, turmeric and cumin; 1 teaspoon dried ginger; ½ teaspoon each of nutmeg and cinnamon; add 2 chopped hot red chillies or ¼ teaspoon cayenne pepper. Be careful not to rub your eyes after chopping chillies – they sting terribly.

CHICKEN CURRY   *(4 servings)*

4 chicken joints
1 clove of garlic
¼ teaspoon cayenne pepper
½ mug plain yogurt
2 tablespoons oil, cooking fat or butter
1 onion, chopped
curry powder as above
medium can tomatoes
½ teaspoon salt

Put the meat in a dish, add the chopped garlic, cayenne and yogurt. Leave for at least 2 hours; this will help to tenderize the meat. Take a large pan, heat it and add the oil or fat. When it is smoking add the chopped onion and cook over a medium heat until it is soft and beginning to brown. Add the curry powder and cook for 5 minutes, stirring all the time. Add the meat, and mix well. Cook briskly for several minutes. Add the contents of the can of tomatoes and the salt. Bring to the boil, cover, lower the heat and simmer gently for 1–2 hours, until the meat is tender.

Curry improves with keeping, so it is a good idea to make it the day before and reheat it the next day. Make sure you bring it to the boil, see page 100.

Serve curry with boiled rice or rice pilaff (see page 62), thinly sliced raw onion rings, Indian chutney such as mango, shredded coconut, poppadums or pitta bread.

Poppadums are sold ready-made in packets either from specialist Indian shops or from some supermarkets and small shops. Allow 1 or 2 per person. To fry them, heat the frying pan and when it is hot add sufficient oil to cover the base to the depth of 1 cm ($\frac{1}{2}$ inch). Let it heat slowly until just beginning to smoke, then raise the heat. Have two spatulas handy, put in a poppadum and immediately begin to spread it outwards using a spatula in either hand. The poppadum will swell and crisp, turn it over and cook for about 30 seconds. Stand upright to drain on kitchen paper. A toast-rack is useful to prop them, otherwise balance them like playing cards.

You could also serve one or two side dishes, such as:

Banana with yogurt   Allow $\frac{1}{2}$ banana per person, slice and cover with plain yogurt, then flavour with a pinch of cumin.

Cucumber with yogurt   Mix sliced cucumbers with plain yogurt and some finely chopped onion.

Tomato with yogurt   Mix sliced tomato with plain yogurt and a pinch of coriander.

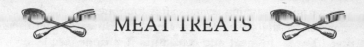

MEAT TREATS

GRILLING OR FRYING MEAT

These are not cheap methods, but at times they are quick and convenient ways to provide a meal for 1 person. Cuts to fry or grill are chicken pieces, chops or steak.

There are one or two simple rules to follow, which will ensure a good result (and therefore guarantee that your money is not wasted).

1. If the meat has been frozen, make sure that it is completely thawed before you cook it. It can be left overnight in the fridge or several hours in the kitchen. It's not a good idea to thaw meat under hot water, which will encourage the growth of bacteria, but you can speed up the process by putting meat under running *cold* water.

2. Before cooking meat, make sure that it has been brought up to room temperature; this means that it should stand in the kitchen for 30–60 minutes. If you cook it when it is chilled, it will be tough.

3. You can tenderize meat by sprinkling it with lemon juice at least half an hour before cooking it. A little pepper and a few herbs added at the same time will enhance the flavour. Don't add salt at this stage: it will make the juices run and will cause toughness. If you add a spoonful of oil at this point, you won't need any additional fat. Don't use a metal plate for this operation, as the lemon juice could cause a chemical reaction, which will spoil the flavour of the meat.

4. The grill or frying pan must be hot before you start to cook the meat. This means preheating the grill (on full) for about 5 minutes or warming the pan on a medium heat for a little less time. Preheating the pan ensures

that the meat will be seared and sealed immediately on
contact with the heat, thus preventing the juices from
running, which would cause toughness.

5. Cook the meat for 3 or 4 minutes on each side, then
lower the heat and cook until it is done (see below),
turning once more.

Grilling or frying times

Chicken joint: 15–20 minutes.

Lamb chop: 8–12 minutes.

*Pork chop: 15–20 minutes. Test by pricking with a knife or fork. If the
juice runs yellow, the chop is cooked; if the juice is pink, cook for a
little longer.*

*Steak (rump, porterhouse, sirloin, entrecote): 3 minutes each side for
rare, 6 minutes each side for medium, 10 minutes each side for well
done (times given are for a 1-cm (½-inch) thick steak. Allow 100–
175 g (4–6 oz) per person.*

*Chops and chicken pieces are also very good cooked in aluminium foil
or paper in the oven: see pages 84–5.*

A ROAST DINNER

*Roasting cuts are not cheap, but once in a while you will want to
indulge. You can salve your conscience, if you feel you are being extravagant, by cooking the vegetables as well as the meat in the oven
(see page 117). If you have no oven you can pot roast your dinner on
top of the stove (see page 111).*

Below are a few simple rules to help to ensure successful roasting.

1. If the meat has been frozen, make sure it has completely thawed before you cook it. Let it thaw, wrapped,
either in the fridge or in a cool part of the kitchen.
Allow about 5 hours per 450 g (1 lb) in the fridge, half
that time in the kitchen. Because of the risk of contamination, it is always best to let meat thaw in the fridge if
this is possible.

2. Before cooking, the thawed meat must be allowed to
reach room temperature, which means standing, once
thawed, for 30–60 minutes in the kitchen.

3. Preheat the oven to the required temperature for 10–15 minutes.

4. Put 2–3 tablespoons oil or cooking fat into the roasting tin and set it in the oven for 5 minutes. Put in the meat and, using a spoon, baste it with the hot fat. (If you have a grid in the roasting pan, stand the meat on this as it prevents the base of the joint becoming over-cooked. If not, don't worry, just put the meat on its edge rather than flat.)

5. Put the meat in the oven on the centre shelf and cook to required time (see below). Baste beef, lamb or chicken every 20 minutes. Pork, because it is fatty, doesn't need basting.

6. At the end of the cooking time, turn the oven to low and leave the meat for 15 minutes. This helps it to compact and makes it easier to carve.

ROAST MEAT

Cuts

There are several different cuts from each type of meat suitable for roasting, some of which are cheaper than others. It really is worthwhile cultivating your local butcher, as he will advise you on which are the best buys at that moment.

I suggest for roasting beef you buy either topside or silverside, which should be well hung, which means it will be a darkish red; the more expensive sirloin and top rib are for real high days and holidays and if you do buy one of these, reduce the cooking time (see page 108) by 5 minutes per 450 g (1 lb).

For roasting lamb, you will find shoulder very good value. It tends to be fatty, so it is worth cutting some of the fat away before you cook it. Leg is very lean and if you are cooking for 5 or 6 people, you will find it a good buy; it's worth watching out for special offers which often happen at the time that one lambing season, say English, is beginning and the other, say New Zealand, is ending. Butchers often have excess stock of the old season and want to shift it quickly. You can also roast best end of neck which is a good joint for two people, or breast of lamb which is cheap but very fatty.

For roasting pork, the cheaper joints are shoulder, sold with the bone or boned and rolled, knuckle end of leg or spare rib. Pork must be thoroughly cooked to destroy any risk of bacterial infection. Test by pushing a skewer or pointed knife into the centre: if the juice runs out yellow, it is done; if pink, continue cooking for a while longer. For crackling, the fat must be deeply scored before cooking. Pour over 2 or 3 tablespoons of oil and rub in a tablespoon of salt.

Quantities

Allow 100–175 g (4–6 oz) per head for a boneless joint, 225–350 g (8–12 oz) for a joint with a bone. Joints under 900 g (2 lb) do not roast very satisfactorily.

ROASTING TIMES FOR MEAT

	Roasting time	*Temperature*
Beef	20 minutes per 450 g (1 lb) plus 20 minutes	Gas 5/375 °F/190 °C
Lamb	25 minutes per 450 g (1 lb) plus 20 minutes	Gas 5/375 °F/190 °C
Pork	30 minutes per 450 g (1 lb) plus 20 minutes	Gas 7/425 °F/220 °C for first 15 minutes then lower to Gas 5/375 °F/190 °C

GRAVY

Pour away all but a tablespoon of the residue in the meat tin, place the tin on the stove over a low heat, pour in a mug of stock or vegetable water. Boil, stirring to mix, and let it simmer for 2 or 3 minutes.

If you want thick gravy, stir 1 dessertspoon of flour into the tablespoon of residue in the pan and cook over a low heat, stirring until the flour is brown. Gradually stir in a mugful of stock or vegetable water and let it boil and thicken.

BASIC STUFFING

Lamb and pork can be boned and stuffed; if you have a friendly butcher, he will do the boning for you. When stuffing a joint, spread the stuffing thinly and not right up to the edge of the meat, otherwise it will burst out when cooking. The meat must be rolled and tied with string. Estimate cooking times based on the weight of the meat plus the weight of the stuffing. If you don't want to actually stuff the meat, you can cook stuffing in a dish in the oven, pour a little of the fat from the meat over it and cook it below the joint for 30–40 minutes.

Cut a slice of bread about 5 cm (2 inches) thick, put it in a bowl and pour over some boiling water. Let the bread steep until it is cool enough to handle. Squeeze out the excess water and mash with a fork. Add ½ teaspoon of salt, herbs, pepper; a squeeze of lemon juice; a small onion, finely chopped; a tablespoon of oil; and a beaten egg.

Variations

For lamb
1 tablespoon fresh parsley and/or 1 tablespoon thyme or mint
1 tablespoon chopped walnuts, or raisins, or dried apricots
3 or 4 chopped mushrooms and 1 tablespoon of thyme

For pork
1 tablespoon sage or rosemary

MINT SAUCE

Mix 1–2 tablespoons of chopped fresh mint with a teaspoon of sugar. Pour over a little boiling water to dissolve the sugar. Add enough wine vinegar or cider vinegar to cover the herbs.

YORKSHIRE PUDDING

Make a batter (see page 138). Forty minutes before the meat is done, put 1 tablespoon of dripping or oil into a roasting or loaf tin and place it on a shelf at the top of the oven. Leave it for 5 minutes, until it is smoking hot, then pour in the batter. Put the tin back into the oven and leave for 35 minutes until the batter is well risen and golden.

APPLE SAUCE

Peel and slice 2 or 3 apples and put them in a small pan with 1 tablespoon of water and a little butter. Cook gently for 30–40 minutes until they are soft. Mash with a fork.

You can add flavour to roast meat by sprinkling herbs or other seasonings over the joint before it is cooked. Lamb responds especially well to this kind of treatment. Use a knife to make slits in the meat and insert slivers of garlic; or sprinkle the meat with ground cumin or coriander or a mixture of both; or smear the meat with mustard; or pour over a tablespoon or two of honey; or sprinkle the meat with herbs such as thyme, oregano and parsley.

ROAST CHICKEN OR TURKEY

Check to see if there is a plastic bag inside the bird containing the giblets. If so, remove it. If the bird has been frozen, make sure that it is thoroughly thawed, with no ice particles inside. Put a slice of lemon inside and a tablespoon of margarine or butter. If you like, add a teaspoon of herbs, such as thyme, parsley or tarragon, and sprinkle the outside of the bird with herbs. Alternatively, stuff the chicken, using the basic stuffing recipe. Spread margarine or butter over the bird or pour over some oil.

To make sure a chicken browns evenly, either baste it every 20 minutes, or start cooking with it on its side, after 20 minutes turn it on its other side, after a further 20 minutes turn it breast up, baste it and leave for remaining cooking time.

If you are cooking a turkey, put a piece of foil or greaseproof paper over it to prevent it browning too quickly. Remove the foil or paper 30 minutes before the end of cooking time. Baste every 30 minutes.

A 1.6 kg (3½ lb) chicken will feed 4 people amply. To estimate number of people for a turkey, allow about 350 g (12 oz) per head.

ROASTING TIMES FOR POULTRY

	Roasting time	Temperature
Chicken	20 minutes per 450 g (1 lb) plus 20 minutes	Gas 5/375 °F/190 °C
Turkey	15 minutes per 450 g (1 lb) plus 15 minutes	Gas 4/350 °F/180 °C Last 30 minutes: Gas 6/400 °F/200 °C

THE GIBLETS

If giblets have been sold with the bird put them in a pan of water. Add pepper, salt, an onion and a sprinkling of herbs. Bring to the boil, simmer for 30 minutes. Use the resulting stock as a basis for gravy or soup.

BREAD SAUCE

Cut a slice of bread 3.5 cm (1½ inches) thick, break it in four and put in a pan with 300 ml (½ pint) milk, and a whole small onion in which, if you like, you can stick 2 whole cloves. Heat it over a low heat, breaking up the bread with a fork. Let it simmer for 5 minutes, add a pinch of salt and some pepper. Cover and set aside for half an hour to absorb the flavour of the onion. Reheat and remove the onion.

POT ROASTING

This is a method of roasting a joint if you have no oven. Cheaper joints of meat, such as brisket, pot roast very well. Generally meat will take about 45 minutes per 450 g (1 lb), a chicken will take about 30 minutes per 450 g (1 lb). Sometimes you will see boiling fowls for sale; these are old laying hens and are cheap. They can be pot roasted but will take up to an hour per 450 g (1 lb). The method is simple.

Use a heavy-based pan or casserole because as only a small amount of liquid is used, a thin pan will burn. First heat a tablespoon or two of oil or fat in the pan, turn the heat on high and brown the meat all over. Pour in ½ mug of stock (add a little wine as part of the stock if you have some available), add some chopped vegetables, such as an onion and a carrot, season with salt and pepper and add ¼ teaspoon of herbs such as thyme or parsley. Put on the lid. This must be tight-fitting. If it isn't, put a piece of foil under the lid or seal it by mixing a little flour-and-water paste and putting a layer all around the rim of the pot before putting on the lid. Cover and cook over a very low heat.

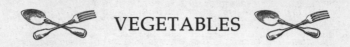# VEGETABLES

You may think vegetables are boring and associate them, as so many people do, with the overcooked, soggy cabbage of school days or with something on your plate which you were told to eat up because it was good for you. A really palatable and well-cooked vegetable is incredibly easy to achieve, however. It needs very little preparation, a minimum of cooking time and just a little judicious seasoning (such as a dab of margarine or butter, some yogurt, salt, pepper and perhaps a sprinkling of herbs or nutmeg) to make it delicious.

Many vegetables are also pleasant eaten raw either on their own – with a dip of, say, mayonnaise or plain yogurt – or as part of a salad (see the chapter on salads, pages 119–125). On the other hand, if you make an extra quantity of basic mince (see page 91) one evening, the following day you could use the remainder to stuff a vegetable (see the ideas on pages 92–3). Consult the index for other main-dish ideas for vegetables which are to be found in various sections of the book.

In order to preserve as many of the vitamins and nutrients as possible, vegetables should ideally be prepared just before use. They should be washed rather than soaked, as prolonged soaking destroys much of their value. However, potatoes will discolour if left in the air for any length of time, so if you are not ready to use them immediately, let them stand in cold water once you have peeled them.

Most vegetables need only a very little water in which to cook. As this water will absorb some of the goodness of the vegetables, it is a good idea to save it and use it as a basis for soups, stocks or gravy.

ROOT VEGETABLES

Allow 100–175 g (4–6 oz) per person. Wash or scrub under running water.

CARROTS

Don't peel unless the skin is very tough. New carrots can be cooked whole; older ones can be quartered lengthways or cut into rings. Try boiling them in just enough water to cover them, with a teaspoon of sugar, a tablespoon of margarine or butter and a pinch of salt. Cover the pan, bring to the boil, lower heat and cook for 10–15 minutes until they are tender. Remove the lid and boil rapidly until all the water has evaporated. The carrots will be covered in a lovely sweet glaze.

JERUSALEM ARTICHOKES

These can be cooked in their skins. Just cover them with water, bring to the boil, add salt, place the lid on the pan, lower the heat and simmer until they are tender. They will take anything from 5 to 15 minutes, depending on size. Drain. They will benefit from being returned to the pan with a knob of margarine or butter. Shake the pan over a low heat to cover the vegetables with a thin coating and add a few herbs such as chopped parsley or mint or a little thyme.

PARSNIPS, SWEDES AND TURNIPS

These should usually have their outer skins removed, although new turnips can be cooked in their skins. Quarter them, put them into boiling water, add a pinch of salt, cover and simmer until tender, they will take 10–15 minutes. Eat with a tablespoon of margarine or butter, plenty of pepper, and chopped fresh parsley, or finish as for Jerusalem artichokes. Swedes are delicious mashed with margarine or butter and pepper.

POTATOES

Choose ones of uniform size, or cut them all to the same size. Cut away any damaged pieces and remove the eyes. There's no need to peel them, especially new potatoes. If you do peel them, remove the skin as thinly as possible, using a peeler rather than a knife – it will be more efficient. Remember much of the goodness is just under the skin. To boil them, put them in a saucepan, cover with cold water, bring to the boil, add a pinch of salt, cover them, lower the heat and let them simmer until soft, 20–30 minutes according to size.

New potatoes should be dropped into already boiling water, this helps conserve their abundance of vitamin C. A little mint added to the water gives them a lovely taste.

Boiled new or old potatoes are delicious with a tablespoon of butter or margarine and a sprinkling of chopped parsley, fresh if you can get it.

GREEN VEGETABLES

Allow 100–175 g (4–6 oz) for 1 person, except for spinach which shrinks a great deal, so allow 225 g (8 oz).

BRUSSELS SPROUTS

Leave them whole, remove the outer damaged leaves and cut off the base, rinse under running water. Cook in about 2 cm (1 inch) of water. Bring it to the boil, add salt, cover and cook over a medium heat for 5–10 minutes. Under- rather than overcook. Drain and add a knob of margarine or butter to the pan, toss the vegetables in this and season with a little extra salt, some pepper and a pinch of nutmeg.

CABBAGE AND GREENS

Remove any outer yellowing leaves. Wash under running water and cut off the hard root. Cabbage can be quartered, greens cut into strips or cooked whole. Cook as for sprouts, above. Cabbage tastes good with a teaspoon of sugar and one of vinegar.

SPINACH

Wash very well as it contains a lot of grit. It's probably easiest if you wash it quickly in a sink or bowl in several changes of water. There's no need to put any water in the pan; choose a large one, put in the spinach and cook it over a high heat, stirring it from time to time. It will take about 5 minutes and needs to be drained very well. Add a knob of butter or stir in some plain yogurt.

OTHER VEGETABLES

CAULIFLOWER

Cut in quarters or divide into florets, removing any tough outer leaves. Cook as for Brussel sprouts. Cauliflower is nice with a little melted butter or margarine mixed with a teaspoon of paprika.

CELERY

Allow 3–4 sticks per person. Wash and trim off any coarse fibres, the swivel-bladed peeler is useful here. Cut into 2.5-cm (1-inch) lengths. Simmer for 10–15 minutes in an inch of water, covered, until soft.

CORN ON THE COB

Peel off the outer green leaves and white fibres. Bring half a pan of water to the boil, add the corn, don't add salt as it will toughen the seeds. Cover the pan, bring back to the boil, lower heat and simmer for 15–20 minutes. Test with a fork; the seeds should be soft, if not cook a little longer. Drain. The corn is nice eaten with plenty of margarine or butter and seasoned with salt and pepper. Eat them by pushing a skewer or fork into each end, it will be less messy than picking them up in your hands. The inner husk is not eaten. If you like garlic, add a little, chopped finely, to the margarine or butter.

COURGETTES

Allow 100 g (4 oz) per person. Small ones can be cooked whole, larger ones cut into rings or sliced lengthways. Cook in a very little boiling water, covered, for 5–10 minutes. Drain them and melt a little butter or a tablespoon of oil in the pan, return the courgettes, toss to coat them and add a sprinkling of thyme or oregano. You can cook a quartered tomato in the butter or oil before returning the courgettes to the pan.

LEEKS

Allow 1 or 2 per person. Cut off the root and all but about 5 cm (2 inches) of the green top. Discard the outer coarse leaves. Leeks often contain a lot of grit. To clean them, slice them almost in half lengthways, hold under a running tap, opening out the leaves to clean in between (or dowse them up and down in a jug of cold water). Simmer the leeks whole or cut into 2.5-cm (1-inch) pieces, barely covered with water, in a covered pan. They will take 10–20 minutes. Drain well and eat with margarine or butter, and perhaps a tablespoon of grated cheese.

RED CABBAGE

A small cabbage will serve 4 people. Cut into quarters, wash and cut away the hard stalk. Shred it and put into a deep pan or casserole with a pinch of salt, pepper, 2–3 tablespoons wine vinegar, 2 tablespoons of margarine or butter. Cover and cook for 1 hour on a low heat. Add 2 quartered eating apples and a tablespoon of sugar. Cook for a further hour. Red cabbage can also be cooked in the oven at Gas 3/325 °F/160 °C. It reheats successfully.

PEAS

Allow 225 g (8 oz) unshelled per person. Shell them. Simmer with water to cover with a teaspoon of sugar and a sprig of mint for 15–20 minutes, or until tender, in a covered pan.

RUNNER BEANS

Allow 100 g (4 oz) per person. Top and tail them and remove any stringy side pieces. Cut into 2.5-cm (1-inch) pieces. Simmer in a covered pan with water to cover for about 10 minutes or until tender. Serve with margarine or butter, salt and pepper.

BROAD BEANS

Prepare and cook as for peas.

STIR-FRIED VEGETABLES

This is a very quick, nutritious way of cooking and is especially good for vegetables. It is based on the Chinese method of preparing meals. You need to use a large, deep pan with a lid made of thin metal which will conduct the heat rapidly. So a wok is, of course, ideal (see page 18), or a multicooker (page 19) lends itself very well to this way of cooking. Vegetables, meat and fish can all be stir-fried, and if you are attracted by this method, it would be worth having a look at some Chinese cookery books.

The ingredients must first be cut into slices or shreds of an inch or two in length. The pan is heated with a tablespoon or two of oil and, when it is hot, to give flavour to the finished dish stir-fry a chopped onion, clove of garlic or piece of root ginger. Stir-frying means what it says, you constantly stir the contents of the pan while frying. After a couple of minutes, throw in the cut vegetables and stir-fry them over a high heat for 2 or 3 minutes. At this point you then add such flavourings as 2 or 3 tablespoons of stock, a few drops of soy sauce, a tablespoon or two of wine or perhaps some sherry or montilla if you have some to hand, perhaps a teaspoon of sugar or one of vinegar, a sprinkling of herbs or spices. At this point such vegetables as beansprouts, celery, leeks, peas, runner beans, mushrooms will be ready. Others such as cabbage, broccoli, cauliflower, Brussels sprouts, aubergine or courgettes will benefit from being braised for 2 or 3 minutes. To do this, put on the lid, lower the heat and leave.

Meat or fish can be added to these sort of dishes. It must be sliced finely in the case of meat or cut into 5-cm (2-inch) squares if using fish. Meat or fish should be stir-fried for 2 or 3 minutes before adding the other ingredients. It's a good idea to coat the fish in a tablespoon or two of cornflour before frying to prevent it sticking to the pan. You can use minced meat or perhaps chicken, rabbit, lean pork, chicken livers. If you have some leftover meat or decide to use canned fish such as tuna or – for a treat – frozen prawns (defrosted first), these should also be stir-fried for a few minutes before adding the vegetables to make sure they are thoroughly heated.

VEGETABLES TO BAKE OR BRAISE

If you are already using the oven, here are some ways of cooking vegetables at the same time. If you are baking or braising root vegetables, they should be of the same size or cut into uniform pieces. They will cook more quickly if you boil them for 5 minutes first before adding them to the dish. Either cook them in the same tin as the meat if you are roasting, or put 2 or 3 tablespoons of oil into a shallow oven dish or tin and preheat it while the vegetables are boiling.

You can roast potatoes, parsnips, turnips and swedes by this method. They will take 1–1½ hours at Gas 6/400 °F/200 °C, depending on whether they have been pre-boiled.

ONIONS

Bake whole without skinning; simply cut off a little from each end and stand on a baking sheet. They will take about 1 hour at the oven setting suggested above.

MUSHROOMS

Large, flat mushrooms can be put into a shallow dish with a knob of margarine or butter or a tablespoon of oil. Season with a little salt and pepper and a sprinkling of herbs such as thyme or parsley. They will take about 10 minutes at the above oven setting (or they can be put under a hot grill for 4–5 minutes).

TOMATOES

Cut them in half; sprinkle the cut surfaces with a little oil, salt, pepper *and thyme, oregano, basil or mixed herbs. Put in a shallow oven dish. They will take about 10 minutes to cook at the above oven setting.*

BRAISED VEGETABLES

Celery, leeks, carrots, swedes and turnips can all be braised. Boil for a few minutes, drain and put into a shallow oven dish with just enough water to cover. Season with salt and pepper and place in the lower part of the oven. They will take 1–1½ hours to cook at Gas 6/400 °F/200 °C.

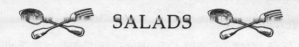

SALADS

The wonderful thing about salads is that you can make a perfectly balanced meal without doing any cooking at all. You can use almost any vegetable and don't have to limit yourself to those well-known ingredients – lettuce, tomato and cucumber. Raw vegetables retain all their nutrients and although they are not a sufficient meal in themselves, all you need to do is to supplement them with say a slice of bread or some potatoes, perhaps a piece of cold meat or a hard-boiled egg, or some cheese, or a smoked mackerel or other fish, or perhaps an omelette. You can have a salad with any hot meal instead of cooking vegetables.

You can eat salads summer and winter using the vegetables which are in season. It is interesting experimenting, but if up to now you've never thought of doing so, here are some ideas to set you off. You'll find some dressings at the end of this section, which are cheaper than bought salad cream and will help to make the salads more interesting.

When making salads, use vegetables which are as fresh as possible to keep their maximum food value and prepare them just before you are ready to eat. They should be washed under running water and not left to soak. There is no need to shred or cut them very finely, except in the case of some of the tougher root vegetables.

AVOCADO PEAR

Although something of a luxury, it is sometimes possible to buy avocados cheaply. They must be eaten soft and so, once ripe, their storage life is limited and often the greengrocer has to sell them off cheaply on, say, a Saturday. Cut them in half lengthways, and remove the stone. Pour some dressing such as vinaigrette, mayonnaise, etc. in the centre, or eat with cottage cheese or fish such as tuna. The flesh goes black in the air, so to prevent this, sprinkle with lemon juice. If you want to save one half overnight, keep the half with the stone, cover it *in clingfilm and keep in the fridge. The stone will help to prevent the avocado from discolouring.*

BEANSPROUTS

Eat them as they are or mix them with, say, chopped apple, onions, chopped green or red pepper, sliced mushrooms. Keep them fresh in a plastic bag in the fridge and sprinkle them with water to help to preserve them. Beansprouts are very nutritious and it is easy to grow your own. You'll find the method on page 145.

BEETROOT

Slice or chop cooked beetroot (beetroot is normally sold cooked). It goes well with yogurt dressing or vinaigrette, hard-boiled egg, chopped apple, tomato, garlic.

CABBAGE

Buy either firm white or red and cut off just what you need, saving the rest. Slice it. Mix with vinaigrette, mayonnaise or yogurt dressing. It goes well with chopped red apple, no need to peel, grated carrot, chopped celery, chopped green pepper, dried fruit, chopped nuts, sliced onion, red kidney beans, parsley.

CARROT

Grate or slice and mix with a dressing, or fresh lemon juice. Nice with finely chopped onion, garlic or parsley.

CAULIFLOWER

Cut off a few florets and mix with a vinaigrette or mayonnaise flavoured with mustard.

CELERIAC

Peel and grate. Mix with vinaigrette or a yogurt dressing.

CELERY

Use a couple of sticks, wash and peel away any tough fibres. Cut into 2.5-cm (1-inch) lengths. Celery goes with vinaigrette dressing or mayonnaise, yogurt, chopped apple, nuts, grated carrot, sliced cheese, cooked potato, chopped green or red pepper.

CHICORY

Wipe and slice. Good with grated carrot, chopped orange, and an oil and lemon juice dressing.

CHINESE LEAVES

A cross between lettuce and cabbage. Cut off just what you need from the top end. Mix with vinaigrette. Chinese leaves go well with the same things as cabbage.

COURGETTE

Slice, chop or grate. Goes well with vinaigrette, chopped onion and grated cheese, garlic, thyme, parsley.

CUCUMBER

Slice or dice. Goes well with cottage cheese, yogurt, mint, chives.

ENDIVE

Looks like frizzy lettuce, and has a slightly bitter flavour. Use like lettuce.

FENNEL

Remove outer coarse leaves and slice. Nice with sliced cheese, grated carrot and a vinaigrette.

GARLIC, ONION AND CHIVES

All add a pungent flavour to salads so watch out how much you use. If you want to add only a mild flavour of garlic, simply rub the salad bowl with a cut clove before adding your salad ingredients. Otherwise chop or crush it finely. Spring onions can be surprisingly strong. Chives can be grown in a pot on a windowsill. You simply cut off a few of the leaves and snip them over the salad with scissors. If you're growing them, it's better not to let them flower as you want all their strength to go into producing food for you. Chew raw parsley to counteract the smell of garlic or onions on your breath.

HERBS

Fresh herbs such as chives, parsley, mint and basil make salads more interesting. It's worth buying some in pots and growing your own.

If using dried herbs with salads, use sparingly as their flavour is strong.

LETTUCE

Wash under running cold water and shake in a clean tea-towel or colander to remove as much excess water as possible. Some lettuce is grown under such clean conditions that you may need only to wipe the leaves with a piece of kitchen paper. A whole lettuce is too much for one person, so break off just what you need and keep the rest in a plastic bag at the bottom of the fridge, or wrap in a newspaper and keep in a cool, dark place. As a change from the usual round lettuce, try Cos, Iceberg or Webb's Wonder – they are all very crisp and tasty and will keep well.

MUSHROOMS

Slice or, if small, leave whole. Mix with vinaigrette or yogurt dressing with a little chopped onion or garlic. Mushrooms go well with thyme, parsley, chickpeas and fish such as tuna or mussels.

RADISHES

Try dipping them in salt and butter.

TOMATOES

Slice and sprinkle them with a little vinaigrette dressing. Nice with basil, mint, chives, parsley, garlic or chopped onion and yogurt.

SALADS WITH COOKED VEGETABLES

If you cook more vegetables than you need for one meal, you can use the rest to make some interesting salads. The vegetables are best if they are cooked until they are just tender. If you add dressing to them while they are still warm, they will absorb much more of the flavour.

BEANS

Mix beans (chickpeas, red kidney beans, haricots, lentils, etc.) with a vinaigrette dressing.

POTATOES

Use peeled or unpeeled potatoes. Slice them and mix with vinaigrette, mayonnaise or yogurt dressing. They go well with onion, chives, garlic, parsley and mint.

RICE AND PASTA

Mix while still warm with a tablespoon of wine vinegar and a pinch each of salt, pepper and nutmeg. Add enough oil to moisten. Just before you eat add, say, a sliced tomato, small pieces of left-over chicken, a small can of tuna fish, some sliced mushrooms, chopped ham or other cold meat, a tablespoon of chickpeas or other pulses or some beansprouts.

RUNNER BEANS, FRENCH BEANS, PEAS

Mix with a dressing such as vinaigrette or mayonnaise. Add chopped onion or chives.

ROOT VEGETABLES

Slice or chop vegetables such as carrots, parsnips, swedes or turnips and mix with mayonnaise.

SALAD DRESSINGS

FRENCH DRESSING (VINAIGRETTE)

Mix 1 tablespoon of wine vinegar or cider vinegar and 6 tablespoons of oil. Add a pinch of salt, pepper and a teaspoon of mustard, either powder or ready-mixed. The easiest way of mixing the ingredients is to put everything into a jar or bottle with a tight-fitting lid and to shake it. Otherwise it will work quite well if you use a cup or glass and mix with a fork. The dressing will keep for days and will be enough for several salads.

It is better to use wine vinegar or cider vinegar rather than malt vinegar, as this is really too strong. You can experiment with different oils. Sunflower, soya and peanut oil have strong flavours; corn oil is mild; olive oil has a wonderful taste but is expensive. You can also vary the proportions of vinegar and oil. This version is quite mild. You will find many recipes for vinaigrette which specify 1 tablespoon of vinegar to 3 tablespoons of oil. It's all a question of taste.

Alternatively, you can use lemon juice instead of vinegar. This variant is especially nice with fish or mushrooms.

YOGURT

Mix plain yogurt with a squeeze of lemon juice, a pinch of salt and pepper, and a little finely chopped onion, garlic or chives. Vary the flavour by adding a pinch of herbs, a dash of Worcester sauce, a teaspoon of curry powder, tomato purée or horseradish, or an equal quantity of mayonnaise.

BLUE CHEESE

Mash 50 g (2 oz) of blue cheese with ½ mug of plain yogurt.

MAYONNAISE

If you buy mayonnaise in a jar, it is better to get one of the special brands or those sold under their own name by supermarkets. Have a look at the label to see what ingredients are listed. A true mayonnaise is made from eggs, oil, vinegar or lemon juice and seasoning.

You may like to make your own. It can be a bit tricky: sometimes it separates and curdles as you make it. You can lessen the chance of this happening by putting a couple of teaspoons of bought mayonnaise into the bowl with the egg yolks.

In a bowl put two egg yolks (see page 146 for how to separate eggs), a pinch of salt, a little pepper, ¼ teaspoon of mustard and a teaspoon of wine vinegar or cider vinegar. (Add 2 teaspoons of ready-made mayonnaise if you have any.) Put ½ mug of oil – use sunflower, corn or soya oil – into a jug or bottle. Using a ballon whisk, beat the mixture thoroughly and begin to add the oil drop by drop. It is important not to stop beating and to beat in each drop of oil until gradually the mixture begins to thicken and look like mayonnaise. You can now add the oil a little more quickly but don't be tempted to pour it all in at once. When all the oil is added, taste, and if necessary add a little more seasoning or vinegar.

If you want to keep the mayonnaise, you can prevent it curdling by adding a teaspoon of boiling water. Keep it in a covered jar either at the bottom of the fridge or in a cool place.

If it curdles while you are making it or later you can either start again with a fresh egg yolk and beat the curdled mayonnaise gradually into this; or put a tablespoon of icy water (you can use a melted ice cube) into a bowl and gradually beat the mayonnaise into this; or put

a teaspoon of made mustard into a bowl and beat the mayonnaise into
this.

Some variations using mayonnaise and yogurt

Mix 1 tablespoon of mayonnaise and 1 tablespoon of yogurt and add
one of the following:
15g (½ oz) blue cheese, mashed
½ teaspoon of curry powder and a squeeze of lemon juice
1 teaspoon of tomato purée or tomato ketchup
1 teaspoon of made mustard
1 teaspoon of herbs

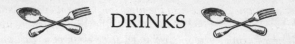

DRINKS

TEA

It's a matter of personal choice whether you buy loose tea or teabags. Loose tea is slightly cheaper but it can clog up the sink. There's instant tea on the market, but it doesn't seem to have any advantages over tea bags and it is more expensive. Tea bags don't need a pot, but neither does loose tea if you buy one of those tea infusers which look like two perforated teaspoons hinged together.

Iced tea *makes a refreshing drink in hot weather. Make it strong, cool it and add ice, perhaps a squeeze of lemon and a sprig of mint.*

Herb teas *are interesting. Less stimulating than ordinary tea, they make a thirst-quenching drink at the end of the day. There are lots of different flavours and you can buy them loose or in tea bags. You might find they are an acquired taste, or that you prefer them sweetened, in which case add $\frac{1}{4}$–$\frac{1}{2}$ teaspoon of honey.*

COFFEE

The difference between fresh coffee and instant is very marked. It really is better not to compare the two. Instant is of course cheaper and for the best flavour buy freeze-dried. See page 29 for how to store it. While most of us know from infancy how to make tea, not everyone is so familiar with coffee, so here are two simple ways of making it.

In a jug: *buy medium-ground coffee, allow 1 level tablespoon of coffee per cup. Boil some water and warm a jug. Put required number of spoons of coffee into jug, pour over sufficient water for the number of cups – the water should be off the boil. Stir and leave for 3 or 4 minutes. To settle the grounds, sprinkle a few drops of cold water over the surface and drag the base of a spoon over the top of the coffee. The grounds should all settle to the bottom but you may find you need to use a strainer.*

Filter: *you need a plastic filter cone; these come in various sizes from one cup to about six. They are used with specially shaped filter* papers, which are thrown away each time, so you have no messy grounds to deal with. Use finely ground coffee, put the required number of spoons of coffee into the filter lined with its paper, stand it on the jug. Pour water just off the boil into the centre, topping up with more if necessary.

If you drink a lot of coffee and find that coffee made in a jug really does produce the best flavour, as many people think, you might consider buying a glass cafetière, which comes complete with its own built-in filter system. The coffee grounds are placed in the base and water poured over; the special filter and lid rest on top; after 4 minutes, the filter is pushed by means of its own plunger to the bottom, thus sending all the grounds to the base. You can buy these in a variety of sizes and it eliminates the need to buy filter papers.

CHOCOLATE

This can be made with cocoa or drinking chocolate. Cocoa is cheaper; drinking chocolate is already sweetened. Carob powder is an alternative with a rather subtle flavour. Follow instructions on the packets.
Hot chocolate with coffee   Put 1 teaspoon of instant coffee and 2 teaspoons of drinking chocolate into a cup, pour over hot milk.
Coffee with chocolate   Make some instant coffee using milk instead of water, grate 2 or 3 teaspoons of plain choclate into each cup.

LEMON WITH HONEY

If you have a really streaming cold, try this before going to bed. Squeeze the juice of a lemon into a cup, top up with boiling water and stir in a teaspoon of honey. Or use an orange. If you happen to have a wee drop of whisky in the house, this will add to the beneficial quality of this drink!

ORANGE OR LEMONADE

In the summer you could save a bit of money on soft drinks by making your own. Put 2 mugs of boiling water in a bowl, add the grated rind – without any pith – of 2 oranges or 2 lemons, add 2 or 3 tablespoons of sugar. Cover and leave overnight. Next day, cut the fruit in half and squeeze the juice into the bowl. Taste and if necessary add more sugar. Strain into a jug. Dilute with water to taste.

YOGURT DRINKS

For very refreshing drinks, try mixing 2 parts plain yogurt to 1 of any fruit juice, or mix yogurt with soda water.

PARTY DRINKS

A really pleasant and economical idea for a party drink is to make a punch or wine cup. You can devise your own mixtures but remember to keep them simple; mixing different kinds of alcohol can result in a literally sick-making brew. A litre will fill about 8 wine glasses.

WHITE WINE AND ORANGE CUP

    2 litres medium-dry white wine
    1 can frozen orange juice
    2 oranges, sliced
    1 litre fizzy lemonade

Put wine, frozen juice and sliced oranges into a bowl. Leave 30 minutes. Add the lemonade and some ice cubes if you have some.

RED WINE AND LEMONADE – SANGRIA

    1 orange, sliced
    1 lemon, sliced
    1 bottle red wine
    1 litre fizzy lemonade
    1 tablespoon sugar

Put all the ingredients into a jug.

CIDER CUP

    1 litre cider – sweet or dry depending on your taste
    1 litre of orange juice
    ½ bottle lemon squash
    1 orange and 1 lemon, sliced
    sprig of mint – if available

Put all the ingredients into a large bowl.

In the winter a hot punch or mulled wine is welcoming. The secret is to remove it from the heat as soon as the top begins to be flecked with white. If you let it boil you will burn away the alcohol. Let it cool a little before serving.

FRUIT PUNCH

- 1 bottle medium-dry Montilla – similar to but cheaper than sherry
- 1 bottle white wine
- 1 litre of orange juice
- 1 litre of pineapple juice
- 1 tablespoon sugar
- ½ teaspoon cinnamon
- strip lemon peel
- 2 oranges, sliced

Put all the ingredients except the oranges into a large pan and heat gently. When top is flecked with white, remove from heat. Add orange slices.

MULLED WINE

- 1 bottle red wine
- 1 orange, stuck with 3 cloves
- 2 tablespoons sugar
- ½ teaspoon cinnamon
- ½ teaspoon nutmeg
- 1 lemon – few strips of peel without pith and juice
- 1 bayleaf

Put all the ingredients into a pan and heat gently. As soon as the top is flecked with white remove from the heat.

BROWN ALE WITH WINE AND APPLE JUICE – LAMB'S WOOL

- 4 litres brown ale
- 1 bottle sweet white wine
- 1 litre apple juice
- 1 teaspoon ground ginger
- 1 teaspoon cinnamon

Put all the ingredients into a pan, adding sugar to taste. Heat gently until white flecks appear. Remove from heat.

NON-ALCOHOLIC PUNCHES

You can make refreshing punches without alcohol. Try mixing a litre of orange juice with one of diluted lime juice, add a litre of ginger ale and top with a few slices of lemon. Or mix a litre each of pineapple and orange juice, top with sliced orange. You can ring the changes by adding fizzy lemonade, tonic or soda water.

SOME NOTES ON WINE

Whole volumes are written on this subject but here are a few hints. Your main concern will be to get the best wine you can at the least cost. Many supermarkets, wine warehouses and discount wine shops sell a very good range of wines which are often less costly than in off-licences. Often they have available very informative leaflets or notices displayed alongside the wine. If you talk to the staff, you will find they are mostly helpful and will recommend reasonable wines to you. Litre or double-litre bottles are good value if you are buying for a party. Wine in cartons is not necessarily cheaper or better.

Red wine should be served at room temperature, which means literally that, so don't stand it on a radiator or stick it in the oven, or hold it under a hot tap; just leave it uncorked for half an hour in the room in which it is to be drunk. White wine is nicer slightly chilled. Below are a few wines which are usually reasonably priced and good value.

Red: *Côtes du Rhône (France); Valpolicella and Barbera (Italy); Rioja (Spain).*
White: *Tafelwein and Liebfraumilch (Germany); Schluck, Riesling and Grüner Veltliner (Austria); Riesling (Yugoslavia and Hungary).*

Only your own taste is going to tell whether to buy sweet or dry wines.

Wine makes you thirsty, so it is a good idea to drink water in between glasses; on the Continent, water is usually put on the table as a matter of course. Drinking a lot of water before you go to bed after a wine session will lessen the risk of a hangover. Headache and nausea are caused by dehydration. If you know you are going to drink a lot without food, try lining the stomach beforehand with a glass of milk.

PUDDINGS AND A FEW SWEET THINGS

This is a section of indulgence. It's for those days when you just have to treat yourself to something or you feel like spoiling your friends: a few ideas for puddings, some breads and easy cakes – nothing very complicated or too expensive. If you have a passion for making cakes and sweet things, vegetarian cookbooks are very good sources of treats that are usually fairly scrumptious without being too unhealthy.

CINNAMON TOAST

The easiest thing of all. Toast the bread on one side only, sprinkle sugar and cinnamon on the untoasted side and put under the grill until the sugar and cinnamon melt into each other. If you have no cinnamon, just make sugar toast.

PAIN PERDU

Beat an egg with 2 tablespoons of milk. Dip bread slices into the mixture and fry them in 1 tablespoon of oil, margarine or butter until golden on each side. Top with jam, sugar, honey or syrup, cinnamon or nutmeg.

POOR KNIGHTS OF WINDSOR

Make as for pain perdu but sandwich a filling between two slices of bread before dipping them into the egg mixture.

BANANAS

Cut in half lengthways and grill or fry gently in a little oil, margarine or butter until soft. Top with marmalade, honey or syrup, or add chopped nuts or dried fruit, cinnamon or nutmeg.

APPLE SLICES

Gently fry slices of apple in a little oil, margarine or butter with some sugar and a sprinkling of cinnamon, nutmeg or mixed spice.

YOGURT

Mix plain yogurt with fruit, grated chocolate, chopped nuts, honey or syrup.

CURD CHEESE

Mix with sugar or honey and some fresh or dried fruit.

SUGARED FRUIT

Peel and slice some fruit, put it in a bowl and top with 1 tablespoon of sugar. Leave in the fridge, covered, for an hour or two. The sugar will cause the juice of the fruit to run, thus forming a syrup.

ICE CREAM

Mix vanilla ice cream with mashed banana and a squeeze of lemon, or top it with a sauce made from 1 tablespoon of honey melted with a couple of squares of plain chocolate, or gently heat 1 tablespoon of jam or marmalade and pour it over the ice cream.

PANCAKES

See the recipe on page 75. If using pancakes from a batch you have made and stored in the fridge, you can fill them and then heat them by standing them on a plate, covered, over a pan of simmering water, or by frying them gently with a little butter, or by warming them under the grill.

Suggested fillings

Lemon juice and sugar
1 tablespoon of jam, marmalade, honey or syrup
Sliced banana with marmalade, etc.
Fruit, such as apple, pear, plum, peach, apricot, etc., peeled and sliced and cooked gently for 5 minutes in a little water or butter
1 tablespoon of chocolate, or chestnut spread, or chocolate hazelnut spread

FRUIT BATTER PUDDING   *(4 servings)*

Preheat oven to Gas 6/400 °F/200 °C. Prepare a batter (see recipe on page 138). Peel and slice 225 g (8 oz) of fresh fruit, such as apples, bananas, plums, cherries, pears, blackberries. Put a tablespoon of oil, cooking fat or butter in a shallow oven dish or tin and place it at the top of the oven for 4 minutes. Put the fruit into the tin, sprinkle over 4 tablespoons of sugar and pour in the batter. Cook in the centre of the oven for 35–40 minutes.

FRUIT CRUMBLE   *(4 servings)*

Peel and slice 450 g (1 lb) of fruit, as in the recipe above. Put it in a shallow dish and sprinkle with sugar. Make a crumble topping (see below) and cook at Gas 5/375 °F/190 °C for 30–40 minutes until the top is golden.

Crumble toppings

Rub 6 tablespoons of margarine or butter into 1 mug of flour and add 6 tablespoons of sugar. Or melt 6 tablespoons of margarine or butter and add to 1 mug of rolled oats, crushed biscuit crumbs or fresh breadcrumbs (see page 145) and stir in 6 tablespoons of sugar.

FRUIT BREAD PUDDING   *(4 servings)*

Peel and slice 450 g (1 lb) of fruit, as for fruit batter pudding. Grease a shallow oven dish with oil or butter. Spread 4 thin slices of bread with margarine or butter and lay them, fat side up, in the dish. Top with fruit and add 2 tablespoons of sugar and a squeeze of lemon. Sprinkle with nutmeg or cinnamon and dot with small knobs of margarine or butter (about 1 tablespoon altogether). Cook at Gas 4/350 °F/180 °C for 15–20 minutes.

BREAD-AND-BUTTER PUDDING   *(4 servings)*

Spread margarine or butter on 6 thin slices of bread. Lay 2 of the slices in an ovenproof dish and add 1 tablespoon of dried fruit, then add 2 more slices and some more dried fruit. Top with the 2 remaining slices. Beat 2 eggs with 1 mug of milk and pour over the bread and fruit. Leave for half an hour so that the bread can absorb the liquid. Cook at Gas 4/350 °F/180 °C for 30–40 minutes. About 10 minutes before the end of the cooking time, sprinkle 2 tablespoons of sugar over the top and return the dish to the oven.

BAKED APPLES

Choose cooking apples weighing about 225 g (8 oz) each. Wash them, cut out the cores and pare a thin strip of peel from around the middle of each apple. Put them into a shallow tin or oven dish, pour a couple of tablespoons of water around them and cook at Gas 4/350 °F/180 °C for 30–40 minutes.

You can stuff the apples before baking them with 1 tablespoon of dried fruit and a little honey, or some chopped nuts, or a mixture of dried fruit and chopped nuts.

BISCUIT FLAN   *(4–6 servings)*

This is much simpler to make than a pastry base. Crush 100 g (4 oz) of digestive biscuits (12 small or 8 large biscuits) in a plastic bag with a rolling pin or bottle. Melt 4 tablespoons of margarine or butter and mix with the crumbs. Put the mixture into a flan tin and press it down over the entire base with the back of a spoon. Put it into the fridge for 30 minutes to set.

You can top this base with fruit, fresh or canned (about 225 g (8 oz) of blackberries, strawberries, raspberries, or 3 or 4 peaches, peeled and chopped). The fruit can be mixed with whipped cream or a half-and-half mixture of whipped cream and cottage or curd cheese. If you use cottage cheese, sieve it first.

SIMPLE LEMON CHEESECAKE

Make a biscuit flan, as above. Put 2 tablespoons of water into a small pan, sprinkle with a teaspoon of gelatine and place over a low heat to melt. Sieve 225 g (8 oz) of cottage cheese – it is easier a little at a time. Add 4 tablespoons of lemon curd and 4 of yogurt and beat well. Stir the melted gelatine into the mixture. Pour on to the biscuit base and leave to set in the fridge for 1 or 2 hours.

CHOCOLATE MOUSSE   *(4 servings)*

Break up 175 g (6 oz) plain chocolate and put it in an ovenproof bowl with a tablespoon of water. Set it in a very low oven to melt – it will take about 10 minutes. If you have no oven, put the bowl into a large saucepan of boiling water – the water should reach half-way up the bowl – and let it simmer gently until the chocolate has melted. Separate 3 eggs (see page 146). Add the melted chocolate to the yolks and beat with a fork until it is well mixed and gleaming. Whip the egg whites (see page 146) until they are opaque and quite firm. Carefully drop them into the bowl of chocolate and yolks and, using a cutting and folding motion, incorporate them into the mixture. Don't stir them or be tempted to hurry this operation, the idea is to keep as much of the beaten-in air as possible. When the whole mixture looks uniformly dark pour it into four glasses. Put in the fridge to set for at least an hour.

LEMON MOUSSE   (4 servings)

For this mousse you need 4 eggs and 12 tablespoons sugar, plus 2 lemons and 3 teaspoons gelatine. Separate the eggs (see page 146). Grate the rinds of the lemons into a saucer. Halve them and squeeze the juice into a small saucepan. Sprinkle in the gelatine and set over a low heat to melt. Put the yolks with the sugar into a bowl and beat them until they are very pale and fluffy, they will go almost white and double in size. If you have a balloon whisk so much the better, otherwise use a fork. Add grated rinds and pour melted gelatine slowly into the egg mixture, beating all the time. Whip the egg whites until they are stiff (see page 146). Fold them into the mixture using the same technique as for the chocolate mousse, above. Pour into four small pots or glasses or into a bowl and leave in the fridge to set. It will take an hour or two.

SUMMER PUDDING   (4 servings)

Make a day ahead as it must be left to stand.

You need 450 g (1 lb) of soft summer fruit such as raspberries, red or black currants, blackberries or a mixture of these. Put the fruit with 6 tablespoons of sugar into a pan, bring to the boil and simmer for 3 minutes. Use a small deep bowl. Cut a circle of bread to fit the bottom and line the sides of the bowl with bread, cutting it to fit. Put in half the fruit, cover with a piece of bread, add remaining fruit and a top of bread. Cover with cling film or foil and put a saucer or plate that just fits on top. Weight it with something heavy like a tin. Put in the fridge or in a cool place and leave till next day. Turn out the pudding by running a knife round the edge and inverting a plate over the top, turn the pudding quickly so as not to lose any of the juice. This is delicious with whipped cream or a mixture of cream and curd cheese.

BISCUITS AND TEA BREADS

DATE CRUNCHIES

> 2 mugs rolled oats
> 6 tablespoons soft margarine
> 6 tablespoons sugar (preferably demerara)
> ¼ teaspoon nutmeg
> ¼ teaspoon cinnamon
> 225 g (8 oz) chopped dates

Mix the rolled oats with the margarine, using a fork. Stir in the sugar, nutmeg and cinnamon. Heat the oven to Gas 4/350 °F/180 °C. Grease your flan tin or a shallow tin dish using oil and your fingers to make sure it is greased all over. Put half the mixture in the dish, and using the back of a spoon press it to cover the base. Sprinkle the dates all over and cover with the other half of the mixture. Press it down firmly with the spoon. Bake for 15 minutes. Remove from oven and while it is still warm, mark it into twelve wedge shapes. Let it get cold in the tin, then cut through the wedges. This is best kept covered in the fridge and served from the tin.

FLAPJACKS

> 6 tablespoons margarine
> 6 tablespoons sugar
> 2 tablespoons golden syrup
> 1½ mugs rolled oats

Put the margarine, sugar and golden syrup into a saucepan and set it on a low heat to melt. When it has melted, gradually mix in the rolled oats. Grease your flan tin or a shallow tin dish, using oil and your fingers to make sure it is greased all over. Put the mixture into it and, using the back of a spoon, press to cover the complete base. Bake at Gas 5/375 °F/190 °C for 15 minutes. Let it cool a little, then mark into twelve wedges. Remove from tin before it gets completely cold or it will stick. If it does stick, put it back in the oven to warm it a little and make it easy to remove. Keep in an airtight container.

BANANA AND WALNUT BREAD

> 4 tablespoons margarine
> 8 tablespoons sugar (preferably brown or muscovado)

1 mug plus 6 tablespoons plain flour (or a mixture of plain
  and wholemeal)
3 teaspoons baking powder
50 g (2 oz) walnuts
2 bananas
3 tablespoons plain yogurt (or a beaten egg)

*Put the margarine and sugar into a saucepan and set over a low heat
to melt. Sieve the flour and baking powder into a bowl (wholemeal
flour will leave a little bran in the sieve, tip this into the bowl). Chop
the walnuts and mash the bananas. Make a hollow in the centre of the
flour and pour in the margarine and sugar mixture. Mix with the
blade of a knife, then add the walnuts and bananas. Mix in the yogurt
(or egg, if you have no yogurt) and mix everything well. Grease a loaf
tin with oil, sprinkle in a tablespoon of flour and shake the tin until the
flour coats base and sides. Put mixture in tin. Bake at Gas 4/350 °F/
180 °C for 1 hour. Cool it for 10 minutes, then turn out of tin.*

PEANUT BUTTER BREAD

1 mug plus 6 tablespoons plain flour (or a mixture of plain
  and wholemeal)
3 teaspoons baking powder
6 tablespoons peanut butter
6 tablespoons sugar (preferably brown)
1 mug milk
2 tablespoons plain yogurt

*Sieve the flour and baking powder into a bowl. (Wholemeal flour will
leave a little bran in the sieve; tip this into the bowl.) Add the peanut
butter and mix in with a fork. Stir in the sugar, milk and yogurt and
mix well, then beat hard for 2 or 3 minutes. Grease and flour a loaf tin
as for banana and walnut loaf, above. Bake at Gas 4/350 °F/180 °C for
1 hour. Cool it for 10 minutes, then turn out of tin.*

*To be certain that these breads are cooked, pierce the centre with a
knife; if the blade comes out clean, the bread is cooked. If the centre is
still moist, cook a little longer.*

　　*Both the breads are better still if kept for a day before cutting. They
can be wrapped in foil and stored in the fridge. Eat them as they are, or
spread with margarine or butter, honey, cheese or chocolate spread.*

SOME BASIC RECIPES

BATTER – FOR YORKSHIRE PUDDING, PANCAKES

12 tablespoons plain flour
pinch of salt
1 egg
8 tablespoons milk
8 tablespoons water

Put the flour and salt into a sieve and shake into a bowl. This helps to mix and aerate them and makes for a lighter batter. If you have no sieve, simply put the flour and salt into a bowl. Make a hollow in the centre into which you break the egg. Add 5 tablespoons of milk and begin to mix in the flour, gradually adding the remaining liquid until all the flour is incorporated. The mixture should resemble thin cream without any lumps. Beat it, using a whisk or wooden spoon, until it is frothy. Set on one side for an hour or two before using – this allows the flour to absorb the liquid, resulting in a lighter finished dish. Beat again before using.

WHITE SAUCE

2 tablespoons margarine, oil or butter
3 tablespoons flour or cornflour
1 mug milk or stock or a mixture of both (you can use
   vegetable water)
salt and pepper

Method 1   Put fat, flour and liquid into a small saucepan. Heat over a medium heat, beating constantly with a balloon whisk, wooden fork or spoon to amalgamate the flour and prevent lumps forming. As soon as it begins to thicken and bubble, lower heat and cook for 2 minutes stirring all the time. Add salt and pepper.
Method 2   Melt the fat over a low heat. Remove from the heat and mix in the flour, return to the heat and cook for 2 minutes, stirring all

the time. Gradually add the milk, stirring to make a smooth mixture. Put over a medium heat and bring to the boil, stirring frequently. As soon as it boils and thickens, lower the heat. Add salt and pepper.

The 2 minutes cooking time is important in both these methods, as it means the flour will cook and lose its raw flavour.

Cheese sauce   Make basic white sauce. Remove from heat and stir in 3 or 4 tablespoons grated cheese and a pinch of nutmeg if you have any. Once the cheese is added, don't boil the sauce as it will become stringy.

STOCK FOR SOUPS

    chicken carcass or giblets, or a ham bone, or leftover meat
        bones
    1 onion
    1 carrot
    herbs such as parsley, thyme, bay leaf
    pepper or 6 whole peppercorns
    3 mugs water

If using a carcass, break it into small pieces. Put all the ingredients into a saucepan, there is no need to peel the onion or carrot. Bring it to the boil, lower heat and cook uncovered for about an hour. If a lot of scum forms on top, remove it and discard. When it is cooked, strain the stock into a clean bowl. Let it cool and then put in the fridge or a cool place until you are ready to use it. Lift off and discard the hard layer of fat that will form on the surface before using.

PASTRY

To make good pastry it is important to keep it as cool as possible. This means mixing it with cold water and to avoid being heavy-handed when making and rolling it. Light pastry needs air, so it is a good idea to sieve the flour and if you are using the first method below, to rub the fat into the flour using only the tips of your fingers. There are several different types of pastry; I am giving a recipe for shortcrust pastry which you will find useful for some of the ideas in this book. Pastry dough tends to shrink after handling, so it is a good idea to set it on one side for half an hour after making so that this shrinkage takes place before it is rolled to the required size. It can be put in a plastic bag in *the fridge. When you roll it out, use light, short strokes away from you. It is important to cook pastry in a hot, preheated oven so that fat and flour amalgamate.*

SHORTCRUST PASTRY   *(for 18-cm (7-inch) flan ring or tin)*

   12 tablespoons plain flour
   ¼ teaspoon salt
   4 tablespoons fat (margarine [soft for Method 2], white
      pastry fat, butter or lard)
   1–1½ tablespoons cold water

Method 1   *Sieve the flour and salt into a bowl. Cut the fat into small pieces and add to the flour. Using a knife, cut the fat into the flour. When it is all coated, use only the tips of your fingers to rub the fat into the flour. Work quickly and lightly until the mixture resembles breadcrumbs. Make a hollow in the centre and add 1 tablespoon of water. Mix with the knife to form a dough, adding a little more water if necessary. (If you add too much, dust the mixture with a little more flour.) The dough should be quite stiff. Dust your hands with flour to prevent the mixture from sticking and form it into a ball. Sprinkle flour on to your work surface and knead the dough for a minute or two to mix it thoroughly. Form it into a ball again and set it aside (see page 139) for 30 minutes.*

   To roll out, sprinkle work surface with flour (about 2 tablespoons), flatten the ball of dough with the heel of your hand. Using a rolling pin, or bottle, roll the dough into a circle, using light strokes away from you, turning the dough as necessary. Watch that it doesn't stick to the surface – if necessary add a little extra flour, but don't overdo it. When it is bigger than the flan tin or ring, fold it in half, put in the tin with folded edge to middle, flip it over to cover base. Gradually ease it to fit, working from middle to outer edges so as not to stretch the dough. When it fits, take rolling pin across top edge to cut away surplus dough.

   See recipes for oven temperatures and cooking times.

Method 2   *Use same ingredients as above. Sieve one third of the flour into a bowl, add 1 tablespoon of water and the fat, cut into small pieces. Using a fork, mash together to form a creamy mixture. Sieve in the remaining flour and mix to form a firm dough, adding a little extra water if necessary. Knead as above.*

DOUGH

Dough is simple to make, but has to be set aside in order to allow sufficient time for the yeast to ferment and grow and cause the dough to rise. It works best in warm conditions, so it's a good idea to warm the bowl in which you are going to make it. You can do this by filling it with hot water and setting it aside for a few minutes.

It is now possible to buy 'fast-action' dried yeast. The ascorbic acid which has been added to the yeast speeds up the rising process. I suggest you use this form of yeast for your pizza bases and bread. Having made a loaf of bread a few times, you will then be familiar with the method and can go on to discover other recipes which you can either adapt to this new form of yeast, or you can make using either fresh or ordinary dried yeast.

Kneading *This is important in order to distribute the yeast evenly and thus allow it to react throughout the dough. The time is usually about 10 minutes. Sprinkle your work surface and your hands with flour to prevent the dough sticking to them. Form it into a ball. With the heel of your hand, flatten the ball away from you, gather it again into a ball and flatten it. Repeat this process, turning the dough to make sure you knead every part. Gradually you will find you are working quite rhythmically. Knead for 10 minutes. The dough will become pliable and elastic and no longer sticky.*

Flour *Ordinary plain flour can be used successfully for pizzas but if you plan to make bread regularly, it is worth buying the special strong flour sold for breadmaking. This type of flour makes a dough which rises well. Wholemeal flour is also readily available. Either use it on its own or mix it with some ordinary strong flour. Wholemeal dough will not rise as much as one using strong white flour; it may also need a little extra water, as the bran tends to absorb liquid.*

PIZZA BASE *(for oven cooking)*

    1 mug flour
    ½ teaspoon salt
    ½ teaspoon sugar
    ½ teaspoon fast-action dried yeast
    ½ tablespoon oil
    2 tablespoons boiling water mixed with 4 tablespoons cold water

Sieve flour and salt into a bowl to mix and aerate, stir in the sugar and yeast. Make a hollow in the centre and add the oil and water, mix with a knife to form a stiff dough. Sprinkle some flour on your work surface and some on your hands to prevent the dough sticking. Form the dough into a ball and knead for 10 minutes (see page 141). The dough should be springy and elastic and not sticky. Roll or press into a ring of 25 cm (10 inches) diameter and set it on a baking sheet. Cover with a piece of plastic which you have smeared with oil – this will prevent the top from drying and a hard skin forming. Leave in a warm place for 30 minutes. Cover with your chosen topping – see pizza section on pages 54–6 for ideas and cooking time.

A SIMPLE LOAF

Double the above quantities. When the dough is kneaded, roll it or fold it to form an oblong. Put it in a 1-litre (2-pint) loaf tin which you have smeared with oil. Cover it with a piece of plastic which you have smeared with oil, to prevent a skin forming. Leave it to rise until the dough has risen above the top of the tin. It will take 1 hour in a warm place such as over a hot stove; two hours in a warm room; up to 12 hours in a cold room; 24 hours in the fridge. These different rising times mean you can if you wish plan your breadmaking to suit your timetable. If you do leave the dough in a fridge to rise, bring it to room temperature before baking it. This means about an hour out of the fridge.

To bake the bread, set the oven to Gas 8/450 °F/230 °C. Bake at this temperature for 10 minutes then lower the heat to Gas 6/400 °F/ 200 °C for 40–50 minutes. Test by removing from tin and tapping the base; it should sound hollow. If not, return to the oven for a little longer. Remove from tin to cool.

YOGURT

If you eat a lot of yogurt, you can more than halve the cost by making your own. There are quite a number of different recipes which you might have come across but for ease of preparation and guaranteed success, I have found the following method the most satisfactory. It involves investing in a wide-mouthed insulated container, which can either be a ½-litre (1-pint) vacuum flask, or a ¼-litre (½-pint) picnic flask; it really depends upon how much yogurt you think you are

likely to eat. You will recoup the cost after making a few batches. How-
ever, you can dispense with this outlay by making the yogurt in a
bowl which you need to cover with a clean tea-towel and set in a warm
place; a warm atmosphere is necessary to maintain the fermentation. I
prefer to use the flask because it is hygienic and compact.

Yogurt can be made with fresh or long-life milk. The milk must be
sterilized and for this reason I prefer to use long-life because steriliza-
tion has already taken place. Long-life need only be warmed. Fresh
milk must be brought to boiling point and then allowed to cool, which
adds about 20 minutes to the preparation time. Using long-life milk
the process only takes 2 or 3 minutes. The milk can be full-cream, half-
cream, semi-skimmed or skimmed; the richer the milk, the thicker the
yogurt.

Buy plain yogurt (not pasteurized) to start the process. Don't be
misled by the name 'live' on some varieties. All natural yogurt is live,
and those with this description are usually more expensive.

> long-life milk, almost sufficient to fill your flask, or 1 pint,
>   if using a bowl
> 1–2 tablespoons skimmed milk powder
> 1 tablespoon plain yogurt (see above)

Put the milk in a saucepan and set it over a medium heat. Make sure
your flask or bowl is scrupulously clean (you can be sure of this by
rinsing it in boiling water). Put the skimmed milk powder and the
yogurt into it and mix to make a paste. Dip your finger into the milk,
it must be blood heat which means you should be able to count to ten
without having to withdraw your finger because it is too hot. Add the
warm milk gradually to the mixture in flask or bowl, stirring all the
time. Put on the lid and set aside. (Or cover the bowl with a clean tea-
towel and put in a warm place, such as an airing cupboard or over a
stove). Check after 4 hours, it should be thick and set; if not, leave an
hour or two more. It can take up to 8 hours but the longer it is left the
more tart it becomes. When it has set, if using a flask carefully pour
the yogurt into a bowl. Put the bowl, covered, into the fridge to cool
and stop the fermenting process.

The next batch is made from a tablespoon from the previous batch.
You can keep on making yogurt almost indefinitely in this way, but if
you find the results are becoming less good, i.e. it is tasteless or too
thin, it is a good idea to buy a fresh pot and start again. You will

probably find that the first couple of batches are less good than subse-quent ones, so persevere – it's worth it!

If you have no skimmed milk powder, make the yogurt without it (it will not be as thick). You can vary the thickness of your yogurt by increasing or decreasing the amount of skimmed milk powder you use.

SOME
COOKING TERMS AND
TECHNIQUES

Baste *To spoon the melted fat or cooking liquids over a dish, usually applicable to roasting meat.*

Beansprouts, to grow *You can buy the seeds in health shops, Chinese specialist shops and in some kitchen shops. The beans you buy must be those sold for sprouting. All the equipment that you need to set you off is a clean jam jar, some muslin and a rubber band. Pick out any discoloured or damaged seeds and any foreign bodies. Soak the beans for a couple of hours, put a thin layer in the base of the jar, pour water over them and then secure the muslin over the top with a rubber band. Lay the jar on its side so that the water drains away. Once drained, put the jar in a warm place, not in direct sunlight, but it doesn't have to be in the dark. Pour over water and drain again in the morning and evening – the beansprouts will be ready in 3–6 days. The secret is not to let the beans stand in stagnant water but also to take care they do not dry out. Eat them when they are at their prime – see instructions on the packets. Harvest them and keep them in the fridge for 2 or 3 days; sprinkling with water helps to preserve them. There are many different varieties you can grow – it's worth experimenting and deciding on your own preferences.*

Boil *Water or liquid bubbles rapidly.*

Braise *Meat or vegetables cook slowly in a small amount of liquid.*

Breadcrumbs, to make dried *Crush toast into crumbs. This is easy if you put it into a plastic bag and crush with a rolling pin or bottle – or you can use a Mouli-légumes if you have one. Store the breadcrumbs in an airtight container for up to a week or so. If you have an electric toaster, the crumbs that collect in the bottom make excellent breadcrumbs. When dried breadcrumbs are to be used as a coating or topping, you could use crushed cornflakes or cream crackers, or rolled oats or oatmeal instead.*

Breadcrumbs, to make fresh *Grate bread on a cheese grater.*

Chop   *Items are cut into small cubes. For vegetables, the easiest way is to first slice, then turn and slice again at right angles. You may find a knife easier to use if you grip it with all your fingers and don't put the index finger down the length of the handle. It's easier to chop rounded things like potatoes or carrots, if you first cut off a thin slice to form a flat base to rest on the board; cut onions in half before chopping. Herbs can be chopped by putting them in a cup or glass and using a pair of scissors.*

Cream, to whip   *You can whip cream very easily without anything more sophisticated than a round-bottomed bowl and a fork. The shape of the bowl is vital as the fork must constantly come into contact with it. Pour double cream into the bowl, tilt it towards you, and whip with the fork which you hold quite lightly with the rounded edge downwards. Use a circular motion, the idea being to lift the cream and so incorporate as much air as possible. If you use a balloon whisk instead of a fork, you can use either whipping cream or double cream.*

Eggs, to hard-boil   *Cook in a pan of simmering water for 8–10 minutes. Remove from the pan and put in a bowl of cold water, crack the shell all over. This prevents a black rim around the yolk. Hard-boiled eggs will keep several days in the fridge.*

Eggs, to separate   *Crack the egg sharply across the middle against a cup or bowl, or use the blade of a knife. Using both hands, carefully open the two halves, letting the white fall into a bowl and keeping the yolk in one shell half. Tip the yolk from one half to the other so that all the white falls out. Or, break the egg on to a saucer. Either use a spoon to scoop up the yolk, or invert an egg cup over the yolk and tip the saucer so that only the white falls into a bowl.*

Egg whites, to whip   *Use the same method as for whipping cream, above. It is vital that none of the yolk or any grease comes into contact with the whites once they are separated. If you are not quite sure whether the bowl is clean, a wipe around with a piece of cut lemon will help to remove any grease. Beaten egg white quickly collapses, so whip it just when you need it.*

Grate   *When grating food using a flat or box grater, it is easier if you use a downward motion.*

Marinade   *Food, usually meat or fish, is left to stand in wine or lemon juice with onion and herbs. This helps to tenderize and give flavour.*

Poach   *Food is put into water and cooked gently over a very low heat, so that the liquid is barely moving.*

Season   *Add salt and pepper.*

Slied   *Food is cut into very thin slivers.*

Simmer   *Water or cooking liquid is just below boiling point; there are only a few bubbles at the side of the pan.*

Slice   *Food is cut into long strips.*

Sweat   *Food, usually chopped vegetables, is cooked over a low heat in fat or oil, without browning, in a covered pan. This method is often used when making soups and helps to release the juice and flavour.*

INDEX

As well as listing specific recipes, this index also indicates those items which are given in the book as ideas and suggestions on basic themes. I hope this will help you to find ideas speedily by showing you at a glance the sort of choices you can make.